YUKON GOLD MYSTERY

YVONNE HARRIS

The Publisher: Argenta Press is an imprint of Dragon Hill Publishing Ltd.

Library and Archives Canada Cataloguing in Publication
Harris, Yvonne, 1935–, author
Yukon gold mystery / Yvonne Harris.

Issued in print and electronic formats.
ISBN 978-1-896124-72-8 (softcover).—ISBN 978-1-896124-73-5 (EPUB)
Title.

PS8565.A6524Y85 2018 C813'.54 C2018-901774-0
C2018-901775-9

Project Director: Marina Michaelides
Project Editor: Kaija Sproule
Map: Byron Kirkham
Cover Image: ©petejau/Thinkstock

Produced with the assistance of the Government of Alberta.

PC: 32

Contents

The book is dedicated to my brother, **Paul Russell,** one of the last living persons to have worked on the paddle wheelers. He was a galley boy on the *Aksala* in the 1950s.

Acknowledgements: Thanks to the Yukon Heritage Branch for the staff's assistance on the Telegraph Trail and to Brian Pelchat, Manager of the Yukon Wildlife Branch, for his expert advice on grizzly bears. I wish to thank members of the Tutchone First Nation who showed me the Telegraph Trail and taught me about their healing medicines. I also wish to acknowledge Pierre Burton who was on a boat trip with me to Yukon Crossing. Thank you to Byron Kirkham for drawing the map, to my editor, Kaija Sproule, and to my publisher, Marina Michaelides.

Chapter I

The S.S. *Klondike*

Victoria found Charlie on the games deck reading Captain Marvel comics with Billy Jack, a dark-haired boy wearing patched denims. The children were travelling on the S.S. *Klondike,* a big paddle-wheel ship that carried passengers and freight on the Yukon River between Whitehorse and Dawson City.

"There you are, reading those comic books again!" Victoria yelled, running along the deck of the big paddle wheeler trying to grab hold of her ten-year-old brother before he disappeared again.

Charlie dashed away, laughing and calling to his sister at the top of his voice, "You can't catch me. I will hide and never come out!"

"Why are you spending your time with a boy from second class? What are you thinking? Next time, I will likely find you below deck with the riff raff of the Yukon, sleeping among the cargo boxes and eating roasted squirrel."

Billy heard this remark. He was used to racial comments, but this time he would not hang his head and walk away. "Youse don't talk about us like that. My Dad works hard at his mine. He don't sit around having fancy meals, but he feeds us lots of good food, like smoked salmon and bannock. We does just fine, Missy." He had olive skin and eyes as black as charcoal.

"Yeah, Victoria," Charlie chimed in. "Billy's family lives on a gold mining creek in the Klondike. Just because they do not have the ninety simolas for first class passage doesn't mean they aren't good folk. In fact, Billy is a right lot more interesting than some of the stuck-up boys in Whitehorse."

"Well, I know he's allowed on the games deck, but just don't let me catch you bringing Billy to our dining room. Speaking of dining, Charlie, it's time to eat. Father told me I was to see you are washed, changed and properly seated at the table."

"Okay, Mother Victoria, but I'm not wearing shorts. Billy's family may be as poor as dirt, but he gets to wear long pants, and he looks grown up even though we are the same age. Shorts make me look like a baby."

"You'll wear your shorts and look like a proper little gentleman. Look, I'll give you a quarter if you just get dressed in your shorts."

"Money? Okay, sis. Bob's your uncle."

"You're learning the worst language from that boy!"

Victoria entered the dining room dressed in a smart navy skirt and crisply ironed white blouse. Her younger brother was now outfitted in his fine blue wool suit complete with the hated short pants. As Charlie walked past a table of elderly tourists, he heard one woman murmured, "Look at the little boy. Isn't he adorable?"

Charlie's expression turned sullen as he took his seat beside his sister. "Did you hear what they said, Victoria?! Can't you understand why boys hate wearing short pants?"

Charlie ate his potatoes then pushed aside his plate, leaving the fish untouched and starting on the dessert with enthusiasm.

"Dad, do we get to Echo Valley today?" Charlie's mouth was full of lemon pie.

"What's that, son?"

"Echo Valley, you know, where the McTavish kids live," Charlie continued.

"Oh yes, our good friends at the wood camp." He was discussing the ship operation with the First Mate and seemed distracted. "You children should accept their invitation to stay there next trip."

Victoria looked at her father in surprise. "Father, don't you remember that we're staying with the McTavishes *this* trip?"

"Did I tell Hector and Anna that you would be staying with them at Echo Valley?" he asked, cupping his hand under his clipped beard, embarrassed to be reminded by his fourteen-year-old about an arrangement any parent should be on top of.

"We'll be at Echo Valley four whole weeks!" Charlie added in an excited voice, "and we're going out on the trapline with Edward and his Dad, and maybe I'll get to hunt with a real gun!"

Victoria hadn't seen her brother so enthusiastic for months. She smiled, thinking how she would enjoy having Mr. and Mrs. McTavish deal with her brother's antics while she found a quiet room in the house to spend each day reading *The Yearling*. It was a book thick enough to last her for the remaining weeks of the summer vacation.

"Hey, Victoria, do you think Edward is too old to hang out with me 'cause he turned fourteen this year?"

"Don't worry. Edward never changes from year to year. For a boy, he's not all that bad. He doesn't get tongue-tied and turn red in the face whenever girls are around, and more important, he keeps an eye on you. Not that I don't like you, Charlie. It's just that I could use a little time to myself. Clara is okay because she is as well behaved as a nun and quiet as a mouse."

That evening, their father allowed Victoria and Charlie to stay up late so they could watch as the ship ran the Five Finger Rapids. They looked on in awe as the river churned into waves of white water as it squeezed through five towering rocks that looked like giant fingers.

Once the sun had disappeared below the horizon, Charlie gave a contented yawn, fell into his bunk and slept until the blast of the horn announced the ship's arrival at Echo Valley. He hastily threw his clothes and his favorite book, *Sherlock Holmes and the Hound of Baskervilles*, in a duffle bag and pulled on a pair of long but itchy wool pants. Before running out the cabin door, he threw the dreaded shorts into the closet. "I'm never wearing these dumb shorts again, and no one can make me!"

Charlie stood next to the gangplank so he could be the first one off. From his perch on the deck, he spotted the McTavish family walking down the hill to the dock. Charlie waved his arms wildly.

"Hi, Edward! It's me! We're gonna stay with you guys!"

As soon as the S.S. *Klondike* docked at Echo Valley, Charlie bounced down the gangplank, weaving his way between the crewmen who were going onshore to load wood. He ran excitedly over to Edward, a teenage boy with a mop of unruly brown hair. Edward had the lanky build of his Scottish father and the dark eyes of his mother. He looked much less like an Indigenous Tutchone than his younger sister, Clara. Nobody would ever think that Clara was anything but Indigenous.

Like Charlie, Edward had not yet figured out that brushing his hair or even getting a haircut once or twice a year was required. While there was a difference of four years between Charlie and the older boy from the wood camp, they had been good friends ever since their two fathers came back from the war and arranged for their children to spend summers together in Whitehorse. But this was the first year the city children were spending the vacation at Echo Valley.

"Hi kid." Edward punched Charlie playfully. "How about you help me load wood, then we'll get you up to the house?"

"I have to help as well," Victoria insisted.

"Girls don't load wood. You're not strong enough, and you would get your city clothes dirty." Edward advised.

Victoria bristled at this. "It's my job to keep an eye on Charlie. I'm careful, and I always help out with chores." Victoria replied icily as she wondered why Edward, who she'd actually liked during their past visits, had apparently morphed into bossy Edward.

"Charlie don't need looking after, do you, Chuck?"

"You mean to say, Charlie doesn't need looking after," Victoria corrected his grammar in a cool tone.

"Yes, exactly, miss. He's too old to have someone hovering over him," Edward replied with a smile that did little to disarm Victoria.

Mrs. McTavish stepped in to halt the argument. "Victoria, would you come with me and Clara to help make sandwiches for the men?"

Victoria looked nervously at Charlie before answering. "Of course, I'll help."

"Thank you, Victoria. You and Clara, wait a minute. Your father wants a word with me before he leaves for Dawson City." Captain Russell had come on shore to supervise the loading. Mrs. McTavish walked over to him.

"Anna, I really appreciate your invitation to my children. Charlie especially needs a mother to straighten him out and encouragement to study like your Clara. I know I haven't been doing a great job with Charlie."

"You do just fine," Mrs. McTavish said. "It's not easy bringing up young ones when there are two parents, and you are left with two children to raise all on your own. We will enjoy having them here, so don't you worry."

"Oh, and before I forget, Anna, I have a few supplies for you. If you go into the ship's galley, the chef will give you a basket of treats for you and the children."

As Mrs. McTavish made her way down the steep ramp towards the ship, the crew leader motioned to the deckhands to hold off for a minute. Edward and Charlie looked over at the ten deckhands, strong men used to slinging wood. Several men took advantage of the break to light a cigarette.

As the trolleys were heavily loaded, the crew bosses kept a sharp eye out to avoid accidents during the brief stops at the wood camps. One of the passengers on shore was a young, slightly built man dressed in a wool suit, his clothes more suitable for a hunting expedition at a castle rather than as a deckhand accustomed to hard labour.

"I'd like to help out with a load," the formally dressed man offered in a clipped English accent. "I am writing about your wonderful northern Canada, and I want to experience everything."

"Sorry, Sir. It's tough work if you aren't used to it. That trolley weighs 800 pounds, and it takes a strong man to roll it down the ramp into the ship's hold. Horace, here, is our trolley man." The crew boss pointed to a six-foot-two, burly man who looked as if he could lift the trolley on his shoulders and carry it onto the ship.

But the Englishman ignored the crew boss and grabbed the handles of the heavy trolley.

"He comes from England," Charlie piped up, pointing at the slim man struggling with the cart, "and I bet he has never seen a woodpile before in his life because his Dad is some kind of king."

"Not a king, Charlie," Victoria corrected. "His father is Lord Littleheart, and they have an enormous mansion, maybe even a castle. They are very wealthy."

"Well, Lord Littleheart has little arms and can't lift the cart."

This remark distracted the Englishman.

"Hold on tight!" the crew boss yelled.

It was too late. Littleheart let go of the handles, and the trolley careened down the ramp. Mrs. McTavish was directly in its path.

"Mom!" Edward yelled. "Watch out!"

There was no time for Mrs. McTavish to escape the speeding trolley. It smashed into her, knocking the startled woman from the ramp. Her limp body flew off the ramp, and she landed on the rocky shore.

"Anna!" her husband called in anguish as he ran to where she lay, motionless.

"Run for the medical officer, Charlie," his father ordered. "Tell him to bring a stretcher, and tell him to hurry."

The captain and Edward rushed down to where Mr. McTavish knelt beside his wife. Her face was ashen, but after her first frantic cry, she did not move or make a sound. She only stared up at her husband, biting her lip from the pain. In minutes, the medical officer had joined them.

"I can't move," she murmured. "My leg!"

Carefully and slowly, they lifted the injured woman onto a stretcher, and Mr. McTavish, Captain Russell and the medical officer moved her into the ship's sick bay.

"You have a bad break on one leg and a great deal of bruising," the medical officer explained to Mrs. McTavish after examining her. "You'll have to go to the hospital in Dawson City to have a cast put on that break."

"I don't want to be in the city without my husband," she said, in a distressed voice.

"Why not come with your wife?" Captain Russell suggested. "The children will be fine with Edward and Victoria, and I will be back at Echo Valley in about a week to check on them. Victoria has always looked after Charlie, anyway, and from what I have seen of Edward, he could take over operation of the S.S. *Klondike* if he had to."

"Well, son," his father said in his Scottish brogue, "can I place you in charge, me boy? You can call on Uncle Joe if there be a problem."

Edward nodded, and Charlie piped in, "I'll help out lots, too."

I have my doubts, Victoria thought, but she held her tongue. As the ship pulled away, she had a sinking feeling that once more she would be left in the position of caregiver to her overactive young brother, a job she despised. Now she'd have to put up with Edward as well, who had become all too sure of himself.

The horn blasted, and the children watched the ship edge out into the Yukon River. In a few minutes the S.S. *Klondike* was out of sight.

"Who's going to do the cooking?" Charlie asked. "I'm hungry."

"The guys will cook," Edward declared. "I make the best steak and potato dinner in the McTavish house."

Victoria's mouth dropped open. Even though Victoria and Charlie had no mother at their house, her father never cooked.

That chore was always left to either Victoria or the housekeeper. Victoria looked Edward over as he carried the suitcases up the hill. He was tall for his age and gangly.

He wouldn't be so bad looking, Victoria thought, *if he just used a little lick and spit on his unruly hair and maybe wore clothes that belonged to the 1950s instead of that bulky mackinaw jacket and the ill-fitting cotton pants that are several sizes too large for him.* The pants were likely his father's, held up and gathered at the waist by a belt.

Clara walked beside Victoria. Although she was upset at her mother's accident, the next best thing to having her mom was to be with Victoria. Today, Victoria wore the latest fashion of pink bobby socks, saddle shoes and a bright pink balloon skirt with matching ribbons in her blond ponytail. Clara wore home-sewn overalls and moccasins with beautiful beaded patterns.

"Could I carry something for you?" Clara asked, smiling shyly at Victoria who was already carrying the basket the ship's chef had given them.

"Thank you, Clara," Victoria replied, handing over a plush bag made to look like a furry cat.

"Is this ever pretty!" Clara admired the soft material of the bag. "The stores in Dawson City have some toys, but nothing like this!"

"My grandma sent it from Vancouver," Victoria said, as they walked up the hill towards the house. "She has been especially good to us since Mom died. My father says we are getting spoiled with all the presents we get. He may be right about that when it comes to Charlie. It seems as if my brother never has enough toys, games or money to keep him happy."

"I wish my parents could get me something new instead of always buying stuff for the trapline or the house. Even then, I'm afraid our place is nothing like the one you have in Whitehorse. We don't even have running water yet and still use an outhouse. We only have electric lights a few hours a day when Dad turns the generator on." Clara was concerned that this older girl might be uncomfortable with their rustic lifestyle.

"I love it here," Victoria said wistfully. "Whitehorse is dusty in the summer. This year it's been even worse in the city. The Americans sent trucks filled with soldiers up the Alaska Highway to Fairbanks, and they all stopped in Whitehorse, making the city too busy and even dustier. It's so beautiful at Echo Valley—no cars or roads, just the river rolling by in front of your house."

Across the grassy yard from the big house were a bunkhouse and a woodshed with a chopping block and firewood piled three feet high along one wall. The McTavish property was neat and organized.

"Let's go inside, Victoria. Mama has given you a room with a view of the river!"

The entrance led into a sprawling living room and kitchen area. The interior walls were logs, sanded and varnished to make the room light even during the long hours of winter darkness. A stone fireplace was the centrepiece of the room, and a winding staircase led to the second floor.

Victoria followed Clara upstairs to a small bedroom. "This is a beautiful house and a lovely room." Victoria sat on the bed and gazed out the window at the peaceful view below.

"Our grandfather helped my dad build the house. They are from Scotland and know all about building houses and fireplaces." Clara felt proud of their house which was the best along the Yukon River from Whitehorse to Dawson City. "There is a washroom down the hall," she continued, "with a pitcher of warm water and fresh towels. Edward will not be long making dinner. He is superfast at cooking and just about everything else."

Victoria lay down on the bed, enjoying the peace and quiet. Despite not having the McTavish parents around, for the moment she felt relieved of the burden of caring for Charlie. *This is so peaceful, but I won't just leave Charlie with Edward all the time. That wouldn't be fair.*

"Chow's ready!" came a booming voice from the kitchen. Victoria woke with a start, for a moment not sure at first where she was or who had called her. As she walked down the stairs, she caught the pleasant aroma of fried meat. The table was piled with food—homemade bread, a steaming plate of steaks and bowls of vegetables. Edward was already seated and dishing himself up.

"Edward," Clara said quietly, "I think Mother would want us to pass the food to our guests first."

"Dig in," Edward smiled, ignoring his little sister. "There's lots."

Victoria watched Edward help himself to four potatoes and two moose steaks. Charlie, who was impressed by Edward's capacity to eat, followed suit, dishing out a pile of food equal to Edward's.

"Charlie, don't take so much," Victoria scolded. She picked out the smallest piece of meat and one potato.

"In this house, everyone gets to eat as much as they want. Since I am the cook, I encourage Charlie to eat well because he'll work it off. Okay, buddy?"

"Okay, Ed," Charlie replied, "and how 'bout you pass me the mouse turds?" He giggled, pointing to the jar of mustard.

"Charlie! How could you?" Victoria railed. "And besides, you didn't even say please." Victoria got up from the table, fixing Charlie with a look that would freeze water. Clara put her hand over her mouth and coughed to conceal a giggle. Victoria's face flushed. "Well, Charlie? What do you say?"

"Sorry, Sis. I just couldn't help myself." He didn't want to get into a squabble and spoil the holiday.

"Sit back down and eat up," Edward ordered. "It wasn't the kind of comment Charlie should use at dinner on the Klondike, but not worth a hanging."

"Alright," Victoria said to Edward, "I will be more than pleased if you take the responsibility of teaching him some manners. I have been trying for years with little success."

"Well, manners aren't high on my list either," Edward said with a smile. "I am more interested in seeing that kids tell the truth, do a good day's work and have a laugh once in a while. Some people take themselves a bit too seriously."

Victoria had little doubt to whom Edward was referring. The mood at the table was tense until Charlie broke the silence. "Don't be angry, sis. We're here for a holiday. Let's play Monopoly after supper. That will cheer us all up." Victoria agreed to play, hoping the game would smooth out the earlier flare-up.

"Monopoly is the neatest game!" Charlie enthused as he held up all the games pieces for his hotels and piles of paper money. "When I grow up, I'm going to be a millionaire and have hotels on Broadway and own railroads and a goldmine and have the fanciest house in all of Whitehorse. I'll get rich without going to school, just like I won this game without being the smartest."

"It is only a game," Victoria said. "If you want to be rich, you need to have a university education and work hard. You'll see."

"Good job, Charlie! I believe you will be rich. But tell me, how will that make you happy?" Edward asked, as he put the game away.

"Nobody will boss me around, and I'd be important. We would have enough money so Dad wouldn't be away all the time, and he could show me how to fish and look after me instead of Victoria."

"Money won't make you into a good person. I'm going to college to become a teacher, so I can help people," Victoria asserted.

"Me, too," Clara added.

"As for me," Edward said. "I'm just going to bed."

Chapter II

The Telegraph Trail

Charlie heard footsteps outside his bedroom.

I bet that's my sister. Next she'll be yelling at me and giving orders, he thought, before turning over and nestling back under the quilts.

But Victoria decided to let her brother catch up on his sleep after his late night on the river. So, when she heard someone moving around downstairs, she jumped out of bed, dressed and joined Edward in the kitchen where he was as busy as a chef at a roadside diner.

"Set the table, will you, while I bang on Charlie's door," Edward ordered in his self-assured manner. "That brother of yours could sleep through a Luftwaffe bombing raid on London."

Why does he think he can boss me around? Victoria didn't quite know how to act with Edward. He had changed. Instead of the friendly boy she knew from the summers in Whitehorse, he was overconfident and bossy. In any case, she did as he asked and set the table, carefully arranging the dishes and cutlery and artistically folding the napkins as if she were setting the dining room table on the S.S. *Klondike.*

Edward bounced down the stairs, taking three steps in one stride. Clara, with her dark hair braided neatly, followed her big brother into the kitchen.

"Looks pretty, Miss Victoria, but we don't use napkins 'cept for Sunday dinners. Too much washing when Mom's not got a washing machine like you folks," Edward said, gathering up her fancily folded table arrangement. "Now pass me your plate, and I'll give you a stack of pancakes."

"Thank you," Victoria replied, "One pancake will do."

"We're going to hike up to the trapline cabin today, so you'd better eat up."

"One pancake, and only one, please," Victoria said icily.

"We're going to bring our lead dog and her puppies down to the big house," Clara piped in, trying to change the subject and bring peace between her brother and Victoria. "Sheba was about to have her litter, so we didn't want to move her earlier."

"Puppies!" Victoria exclaimed. "That will be nice. How far is it to the trapline cabin?"

"About six miles one way. We'll sleep there tonight," Edward said as he flipped a pancake in the air and passed it to Victoria on a warmed plate. "One McTavish pancake for the mademoiselle from the big city."

"Charlie! Get down here, or I'll drag you out of bed," Edward yelled up the staircase. Victoria noticed his voice had changed. He sounded a lot like his dad, and he was definitely acting differently.

A few minutes later, a sleepy-eyed Charlie, still in his pajamas, shuffled down the stairs.

Although the pancake was delicious, and Victoria would have liked to have another, she was embarrassed to ask for more since she'd made such a fuss about only having one. Clara and Charlie did not have any qualms about eating their share, and they kept Edward busy at the stove.

Victoria and Clara tidied up the kitchen and looked for jackets and shoes for the hike, while Edward and Charlie packed food for the trip up the hillside.

"Hey, Ed, how do you get your food? I mean corn flakes, cookies and stuff like that?" Charlie asked as they added snacks, bottles of water and insect repellent to the backpacks.

"Buy cookies or fancy cereal?" Edward replied with a laugh. "Heck no! Mom bakes everything we eat, and the only time I've had store-bought cookies or corn flakes was at your house in Whitehorse. For supplies like sugar, flour and oat meal, we take the motorboat down to the Hudson's Bay Store at Fort Selkirk and get everything in huge bags."

"Hot cereal! Yuk! Our housekeeper tried to make me eat porridge once, and I nearly barfed."

"Well, kid, if you stay with us for the rest of the summer, you'll be eating porridge or starving 'cause I don't make pancakes every morning."

"I guess living up here in Echo Valley is nothing like Whitehorse," Charlie observed. "This is the real wilderness, just like those old stories by that guy who lived during the Klondike Gold Rush. Hey, Victoria, who's the guy who wrote about the dog?"

"Jack London," she replied. "He wrote *Call of the Wild* in 1903 a few years after he joined the Klondike Gold Rush. Youngsters and adults all over the world read his book." Victoria spoke as if she was already in front of a class of students.

"Mom doesn't let me read his books because Jack London said nasty things about our people," Clara added shyly.

"I didn't realize that." Victoria was surprised to hear a ten-year-old make a comment on literature.

"Well, that's him anyway," Charlie continued. "Your family hunts for food, you chop your own wood and live just like the miners that guy wrote about back when there were thousands and thousands of gold diggers rushing to the Klondike hoping to hit pay dirt and go home with millions. But how does your dad make money to buy food and clothes and stuff?"

"We do okay. Cutting wood for your dad's ship pays well and then we sell pelts from the animals we trap. Lynx bring a pretty good price, same as beavers."

"You kill beavers?!" Victoria exclaimed, horrified.

"Yes, Missy and proud of it. And how do you think the cows and chickens end up on your plate? I suppose you think they commit suicide? Someone kills them so you can eat, and we kill beavers so we can eat."

"That's different. Cows and chickens are raised for food; beavers live in the wild," Victoria argued.

"Personally, I don't grasp the difference. Anyway, we're not going to agree, and that's enough gabbing. Time to get truckin'. Remember, Clara, the trail is muddy in places, so make sure you and Victoria have wool socks and good boots."

The August sun was dazzling as they started up the trail that wound behind the house. Charlie followed Edward like a faithful puppy while Clara and Victoria trailed behind, chatting as they made their way into the forest.

They had only been hiking for a short time when the narrow forest trail opened out onto a well-trodden path with telegraph wires strung along the trees.

"What are these wires doing in the middle of nowhere?" Victoria asked, looking up where she could see green glass globes the size of large eggs attached to the wires.

"This is the Telegraph Trail," Edward explained. "It was built during the gold rush. Soon after all those gold miners arrived in Dawson City in 1898, the first thing they wanted was a telegraph line so they could send messages to their families in southern Canada and the United States. I think it got shut down because someone built a cable under the Atlantic Ocean. But now people who can't afford the passage on your dad's ship use parts of the trail to get from Whitehorse to Dawson City."

Edward stopped to take a drink from his water bottle. "My dad and I walked to Dawson last year—one hundred and fifty miles—and it took us five days. Let's see. How many miles is that a day?" Edward pushed a wayward strand of hair out of his eyes and pondered.

"Thirty miles a day!" Victoria answered. "You can't be serious. I could never walk that far. I'm tired already, and we've just started."

"Next time eat your breakfast like a good girl," Edward said with a smile. Although he offered the comment in a chiding, friendly way, it made Victoria want to throw something into his self-satisfied face. For the first time in her life, Victoria was the one who was tongue-tied. She fumed, and despite her blistering heels, picked up the pace.

"I ate as much as Edward, and I'm not tired at all," Charlie boasted.

"I'm finding it tough, but when I get bigger I will be able to run up the trail like Edward," Clara added.

"We'll all make it to the cabin," Edward assured them.

"I might not be great at hiking, but I can paddle a canoe, and I bet I can do something you can't do," Victoria said, trying to put Edward in his place. "This summer I took a canoe course from an expert. We tipped the canoe in the middle of the river. Then he showed me how to dive under the canoe and flip it right side up. It's called Buster's Roll."

"Remember, I live on the river, so I learned that when I was Charlie's age," Edward said. "Maybe next time we take a canoe trip, I'll tip you into the river and see if we can roll the boat up."

"I guess there's nothing you don't do better than I." She avoided adding that she certainly wouldn't go on a canoe trip with such a know-it-all. Victoria was in a black mood as they continued up the trail.

"How much farther?" Charlie asked.

"Oh, I don't know. Maybe ten hours, maybe twelve."

"He's teasing you," Clara interrupted. "I know the trail. It's not that far."

They continued along the Telegraph Trail, their pace a little faster on the well-trodden path. Charlie busied himself spotting the green insulators that connected the telegraph wires. Victoria was in the lead, gritting her teeth because every step sent pain up from her blistered heel. She would show him that she could not only keep up but set the pace.

"Whoops!" she exclaimed, almost bumping into two men walking towards them.

"What are you kids doing? Hiking to the Klondike?" the bigger of the two asked, flashing a scary-looking grin.

He was a hefty, grisly-looking man with a crown of rusty, stringy hair and a ragged beard. His head and neck were huge. He continued to grin at the children, but there was little warmth in his smile or his cold, blue eyes.

In contrast, the other man was thin and wiry with a moody face. He looked like he had learned what it takes to be mean, sizing up the children with a shifty gaze. It seemed like they hadn't enjoyed the comforts of civilization for some time.

"We're going to our trapping cabin. And where are you two going?" Edward asked.

"We're headin' for Yukon Crossing if we can make it," the burly red-head replied. "Zeke and I had enough of this blasted country and everyone in it. Our partner took off with our gold poke, and we got nothin' to show for a year's work. He's a tall guy with a black beard. Did you happen to see him?"

"Nope. You're the first travellers we've come across. But a thief can't get too far in this country. There are no roads out of Dawson City, just this trail and the river, so the Mounties don't have a lot of trouble catching criminals. As they say, 'the Mounties always get their man,'" Edward said with a chuckle.

"Sure pulled a fast one on us," the big man continued. "We were camped up the trail when I woke up in time to see him headin' off with our gold. Tried to stop him but instead ended up gittin' my arm slashed." He had his arm cradled against his chest. "We haven't seen his tracks for a while, so I figured he turned up that little trail a ways back."

"That's the trail to our trapline cabin!" Clara exclaimed. "Edward, he may be there, and he's dangerous. Maybe we shouldn't go there."

"Na, don't you worry, little missy. He won't hurt a bunch of kids. He has a couple of kids hisself. Surprised me that he would have stole our poke. By the way, the name's Red," he said, "and this here's my partner, Zeke."

Edward introduced himself and the three others. He shook hands with Red. When Edward offered to shake Zeke's hand, the lean, moody man turned and headed down the trail.

"Zeke ain't used to company," Red explained. "We bin spending too much time at our mining claim, and he got hisself a case of cabin fever. He ain't much good at socializin'. We better mosey along. It's a long hike to the crossing."

"I'd be worried about those two," Victoria told Edward after the two miners headed south on the Telegraph Trail. "Why are you so intent on being friendly with strangers? That's something we would never do in Whitehorse."

"That's how people are along the river. No one passes our door without Mom offering them a bite to eat and, if it is evening, a comfy bed. Makes me happy I live out here and not in the city. Okay, gang, here's where we turn off and climb a few hills up to the cabin."

The branch trail was steeper, winding through the trees and up out of the valley.

"When will we get there?" Charlie asked, as he puffed up a steep hill.

"At this pace, it will be after supper. If you would stay on the trail, Charlie, and if the girls would stop chatting and walk a bit faster, we could get there much sooner," Edward answered.

"That's another four hours!" Victoria groaned.

"I guess this is not the country for Miss Victoria. Maybe if you had eaten your pancakes, you wouldn't be so exhausted."

Edward said this without malice, but when he noticed the stormy look on Victoria's face, he realized his easygoing banter was not well received.

Before Victoria could think of a reply, Clara came to her defence. "Don't you dare make fun of Victoria, Edward. She's our guest, and you should mind your manners."

"Now I am going to have a lesson in manners as well," Edward laughed. "All right, I will slow down the pace."

When they left the ridge, the trail wound down into a small gully. Soon they were in the thick brush and willows in the dip of the ravine.

Victoria slapped at the bugs landing on her face. "Wow, these mosquitoes are so thick I have to keep my mouth closed, or I'll swallow them!"

"Just pretend they aren't there, and they won't bother you," Edward replied in that know-it-all voice that had grated on Victoria from the moment they'd arrived.

"Yeah," Charlie piped in, "they don't bother me neither."

"Then why do you have welts on your neck the size of cherries?" Clara laughed. "I have some mosquito repellent that might help. Do you want me to put a little on the back of your shirt, Charlie, so you'll have some blood left when we arrive at the cabin?"

"Well, okay," Charlie said, pretending not to be bothered by the dozens of mosquitoes on his face and hands.

"Why didn't you plan this as a two-day trip, or maybe a week-long journey?" Victoria complained.

"I have to admit that the trip is easy for me because my dad and I have been taking turns running up this trail to feed Sheba every day for the past two weeks. I understand that it can be a difficult hike if you aren't used to it."

"It's not too far for me," Charlie said unconvincingly.

"Good man!" Edward smiled.

"Don't worry, Victoria," Clara said. "We'll make it. Edward just likes to show off since he is so big, and the rest of us are pipsqueaks."

Victoria could just imagine what Edward thought about her—a wimpy girl from the city. *Well, I'll show him. He won't hear me complaining about anything no matter how much I hurt.*

It was a difficult promise to keep. Victoria had a blister the size of a mushroom on one of her heels, causing her to wince with every step. She was not the only one suffering. Clara also wore light tennis shoes, which were inappropriate for the tough hike, and Charlie, who had spent too much time running off the trail, pretended he was strong but lagged behind.

As the trail curved up a ridge, Edward's pace quickened and Clara began running along a well-worn path.

"It's just around the corner. We're almost there!" Clara yelled as she disappeared down the trail.

"I bet we're not there," Charlie grumbled. "People always think they recognize the trail, and then they find out it's all a mistake and have to admit there are three more mountains to climb, a lake to swim and a river to cross."

"Not this time," Victoria said. "Look! There it is!"

Chapter III

The Trapline Cabin

The log cabin was nestled among the fir trees. A stream trickled through the gully nearby. Clara had already reached the cabin.

"Sheba! Sheba!" Clara examined the dog kennel, and in a panic, called to Edward. "The gate's open, and Sheba's gone!" Clara cried, bursting into tears.

"I am dead sure we closed the gate when we left her. Sheba! Sheba! Come on girl!"

"We have to find her," Clara sobbed. "She has pups now, and they might all be killed by bears, and Sheba needs food so she can nurse her babies."

"We'll find her. Let's put our packs in the cabin and start searching."

"We'll help," Victoria offered.

"Heck!" Edward yelled angrily as he stepped into the cabin. "Look at this mess. That thief's been here. He must have opened the gate and chased Sheba away."

The children groaned when they saw the mess in the cabin.

"What kind of person leaves dirty dishes and drops food on the floor?" Victoria yelled.

"A bad guy!" Clara answered, tears brimming in her eyes. "I'm scared, but I have to find Sheba."

"We'll make sure you are never alone," Edward said in a comforting voice. "I think we should walk up the trapline trail. Clara and Charlie, you two fan out on the left trail, and I'll check the trail on the right. Victoria, you look tired. Why don't you stay and try to clean up?"

"I'm not tired, and I am not anybody's housewife. I'm coming, too."

"Okay. Come with me, but keep up."

Victoria fumed. *One more remark like that, and I will slap his smug face.* Then, trying to be civil, she replied, "I'll be right behind you. Two pairs of eyes are better than one."

The four ran up separate trails calling for Sheba until their voices were hoarse and their energy sapped. Tired, and with Clara still in tears, the children plodded back to the cabin.

"Hey, team, we won't find Sheba tonight, so let's check out the supplies," Edward suggested as they piled wearily into the cabin. "Me and City Girl will clean up the place and get supper started. I'm famished."

"My name's Victoria," she pouted angrily, "and it's incorrect grammar to say 'me will get supper.'"

"Well, Victoria Russell, I meant no harm. You'll just have to get used to my attempts at humour."

The two younger children flopped down on the cots while Edward and Victoria looked through the cupboards. Clara tried to stem her crying, but every few minutes, she uttered a muffled sob. Before long, the tired girl fell into a fitful sleep.

"All he left is a bag of cream of wheat, and dried beans. Not exactly my favourite supper food," Victoria exclaimed.

"Instead of spaghetti and tomato sauce, we'll have cream of wheat. It's getting closer to morning all the time, so I'll cook you some breakfast," Edward said, trying to humour Victoria out of her icy mood.

Building a fire in the wood stove, boiling water and cooking porridge took Edward and Victoria over an hour. By the time supper was ready, Charlie was also fast asleep.

"Let them sleep," Edward said, covering his little sister with a blanket. "They can eat in the morning. Do you want a delicious bowl of hot cream of wheat?"

"I'll pass," Victoria replied, before climbing into the bunk above Clara.

"Goodnight," Edward whispered. "Don't let the bedbugs bite."

"You're kidding, aren't you?" Victoria asked anxiously.

"Right you are, girl. Mom wouldn't let a bug within a mile of our house or this cabin. Sleep well."

Before climbing into the bunk above Charlie, Edward ate a generous bowl of porridge and then put beans in a pot to simmer on the wood stove overnight. The fire crackled and eventually died down.

"It's him!" Victoria whispered nervously. "Edward! Wake up. He's at the door! Listen. Don't you hear him?"

"Who?" Edward woke in a sleepy daze.

"The thief, Edward! Get the gun. You have a gun, don't you?"

"You're having a nightmare. Go back to sleep," Edward grumbled as he turned over and tried to go back to sleep.

Victoria crept over to Edward's bunk and shook him violently. "Get up! I'm telling you there's someone out there."

Edward shook himself awake and listened. "Okay, okay. I'm up, but please don't wake the kids. Clara was upset enough over Sheba."

As Edward rolled down from the bunk he heard a distinctive noise at the door as if a wounded man was trying to get in.

"Okay, I believe you. Stay close to the kids." He quietly removed a floor board, lifted out a rifle and tiptoed to the door.

"Be careful," Victoria whispered.

Edward slowly turned the knob, his heart pounding against his ribs. Holding the rifle in his right hand, he threw open the door with his other hand and pointed the gun out into the black night. No one was there. Then he looked down and saw Sheba on the doorstep with her three puppies.

"Sheba!" Edward hugged his dog and lifted the puppies into the cabin, placing them on a carpet.

Clara and Charlie awoke and stumbled out of bed. Clara cried tears of joy as she hugged Sheba, relieved that her beautiful husky was home safe. Edward fetched the dog food and smiled as Sheba gobbled her meal before settling down to nurse her puppies.

The four returned to their bunks and slept soundly in the cozy room until Charlie woke the next morning.

"Edward," Charlie said, shaking the older boy, "you've slept in. I'm hungry."

"Throw some wood in the stove, kid. I'll be up in a minute."

Charlie added wood, stirred the embers and got the fire burning hot, then sat next to the stove, enjoying the warmth. When Edward lifted the lid on the pot of beans, a rich aroma wafted through the room.

"Yum." Edward said. "The beans are ready."

"I can't eat beans for breakfast," Charlie protested.

"Okay, how about I warm up the porridge from last night."

"Is that all we have to eat?" Charlie groaned, as he rifled through the cupboards.

"I'll show you what a great breakfast cold cream of wheat makes. Stick that frying pan on the stove and slap a spoonful of lard in it."

Charlie followed instructions and watched Edward's every step. Edward dropped a couple of patties of the cold cream of wheat into the sizzling pan.

"Mmm. It sure smells good," Charlie observed.

Edward lifted one of the golden-brown patties onto a plate and set a bottle of syrup on the table. Charlie gobbled down his breakfast and came back for more.

"Now that you know there is something as tasty as Kellogg's Corn Flakes, you can give the beans a try."

Edward and Charlie were on their second bowl of beans when the girls woke up and joined them. Edward had flavored the beans with spices and added syrup to make a delicious sweet dish for breakfast. Victoria, who usually turned her nose up at the thought of beans, enjoyed a second helping. The long sleep put her in a better mood. For a minute, she forgot how Edward's superior attitude and constant chiding grated on her.

"My dad won't believe that I've eaten beans for breakfast," Victoria said, scraping up the last spoonful from her bowl. "Do you know what we ate for breakfast on the S.S. *Klondike*? Eggs Benedict. The chef poaches eggs and serves them on toasted buns with a slice of ham and lemon sauce."

"I think I prefer porridge and beans," Edward replied. "And you will be stronger on the hike now that you have a good breakfast to propel you."

For a couple of minutes, I was ready to forgive him for being so irritating, but one more bossy remark like that, and I'll kick him in the shins.

The four children gathered their belongings, put away the sleeping bags and washed the dishes.

"Hey, Ed," Charlie yelled as he scooped his shoes out from under the bed. "Look at this! There's blood on the floor." He examined a dark smear next to the bed.

"I guess it was the guy that stole their poke. He must have been hurt when Red tried to catch him. Then the thief spent the night here." Edward tried to reason it out but still looked perplexed.

"Maybe it was Red. Remember, he had a cut on his arm," Charlie added.

"I didn't care for the look of those guys. A couple of good-for-nothings in my opinion. Right, Clara?" Victoria gave the younger girl a hug when she noticed Clara's frightened look.

It was a sunny, hot day that grew warmer as they dropped into the valley. It wouldn't be a fast trip, as Sheba's three puppies would have to be carried and given to their mother to nurse at least a couple of times during the journey.

After about an hour, the puppies started to whimper. Edward called a halt, and they placed the hungry puppies with Sheba.

While the others sat on logs, resting and talking, Charlie grew restless and took off running down a game trail.

When Sheba's puppies fell asleep, they were gathered up and gently cradled for the walk down to the big house.

"Charlie!" Victoria called. "We're leaving!" There was no answer and no sign of the ten-year-old.

A shrill whistle pierced the air. Edward was startled at the sound and surprised that Victoria, a city girl, could have developed a whistle that a street boy would be proud of.

"That's neat," he said. "Maybe later you could show me how you do that."

"I need a loud whistle to keep Charlie in tow. We often play hide and seek on the ship, and sometimes I can't find him. Charlie and I agreed that if I blow the whistle once he is to come immediately, but if I give three blasts, one long, one short, one long, like an SOS, he should stay hidden. Charlie can be stubborn, so it doesn't always work, especially if I am trying to get him to get dressed for dinner."

"Why would you want to have him stay in his hiding place?" Clara wondered.

"Just in case. I've been responsible for Charlie since he was six, and I used to have nightmares that someone would hurt him. We decided on a code that I could use to tell him to hide from anyone who might hurt him. He is not to come out until I whistle again, but only once. I know it's silly," Victoria went on, "but I was pretty young when my mother died, and I worry about Charlie."

Victoria gave another single whistle, and Charlie came running at full speed.

Charlie looked nervous. "I'll be back in a flash. I dropped something in the bush. Go ahead, and I'll catch up with you."

He was holding his hand on the front of his jacket as if he was concealing something. He grabbed his backpack and dashed into the bush. The others looked puzzled.

"What's going on with your brother?" Edward asked.

"Is he always so mysterious?" Clara added.

"No way! He's as easy to figure as a Grade One Reader. I don't know what's got into him today."

They turned to watch Charlie run out of the bush. He was no longer holding the front of his jacket, and his pack was on his back. Gone was his customary chatter.

The trip back to the big house was downhill and much easier than yesterday's hike up the hillside. The troop stopped once more to let Sheba nurse the puppies, allowing the four to rest. When they resumed the hike, Victoria and Clara kept up a good pace and soon spotted the red roof of the big house.

Chapter IV

The Big House

As they got closer Sheba bounded towards the house, barking.

"Git off me! Call your dog!" Sitting on the porch of the big house were the two men they had met yesterday. Red was cradling his injured arm, crudely wrapped in a bloodied shirt.

"Sheba! Here!" Edward yelled, and the dog ambled back to him.

Red walked up to the children. "Glad to see you kids. We started on the trail to Yukon Crossing, but I must'a lost my knife back in our last camp, so Zeke hung out here while I doubled back to check it out. Then my arm felt pretty bad, and I figured I couldn't make it to the Crossing. We've been waiting for the Mrs. and Mister of the house to ask if we could rest up for a couple of days till I git better. Hope you don't mind that we slept in your bunkhouse last night." Both Red and Zeke seemed to be sizing up the four children as if there was something else on their minds other than Red's injured arm and the missing knife.

"I bet that crook of a partner of yours took our food," Edward said. Then he wondered if these two were involved in the theft. There was just something about the two men that didn't add up. "Were you up at the cabin with him?"

"You better not be the ones who stole the food because we had to eat beans for breakfast and porridge for supper," Charlie blurted out.

Zeke put his head down while Red flashed a scarecrow smile and looked Edward in the eye. "No way, kids. It must'a been John. We were camping where the two trails met, and John took off early that morning. I chased him up the trail, so he must'a broken into your cabin and then took off with our gold and the food. If I ever catch up to him and git my gold back, I'll bring you the dough for your supplies."

"We ain't coming back this way, I reckon," Zeke said quietly, "but maybe we can send you the money." This was the first time Zeke had spoken.

"Maybe I'll be back; maybe I won't," Red interjected. "Right now, I need some bandages for my arm."

"Clara," Edward said, "you know where Mom keeps the first aid kit. Can you fetch it and, Victoria, could you bandage his arm?"

She didn't like being ordered around by Edward, but this was a task she didn't mind. "Come in the house, Mister," Victoria said with authority. "We'll get you to sit on a chair while I fix your arm, and you'll be better in no time."

As Victoria led the big miner into the kitchen, Zeke started walking up the trail.

"Where are you off to?" Red yelled.

"Just thought I would walk back to our camp and have another look for that knife you lost."

"You don't need to be doin' that," Red yelled. But Zeke kept walking. Either he didn't hear Red or intended to ignore him. He walked in long strides, almost running down the trail as if he was heading for the gold at the end of the rainbow and was afraid it would disappear before he got there.

Victoria cleaned and dressed Red's wound, speaking to the rough-looking miner in a motherly voice. "Now this will hurt," she cautioned, as she dabbed the wound with a clean pad dipped in warm water. "Good. I'm glad you're brave. Next, we have to put on the iodine, and that really will hurt, so just clench your teeth and it will be all over in a minute."

"Boy she sounds mushy, doesn't she?" Charlie told Edward as the two boys walked across the yard to get wood for the stove. "Now you can see why she drives me around the bend. She thinks she's the boss, no matter who she's talking to. It could be a criminal she's bossing around or a murderer."

"Why do you say that? Are you suspicious of these guys?" Edward asked.

He didn't answer for a minute. "Nah, why should I think they're lying?" Then he changed the subject. "You know, Edward, other than our father, you are about the only person I know who seems to carry any weight with Victoria. I'm the only boy in our family; she should have to listen to me, not boss me around."

"When you're older, kid," Edward said, giving him a friendly punch.

Later, Clara and Victoria peeled potatoes and carrots to go along with the chicken Edward was frying. Charlie was given the chore of keeping the fire burning hot in the wood stove. Zeke had returned, and there was an uncomfortable tension around the table, although Red tried to keep the conversation going.

"So, where are your folks?" he asked.

"They're in…" Clara began.

"Mom and Dad will be back soon," Edward interrupted. "They're just visiting. They shouldn't be long now. You know who my Dad is, I guess. He won the army sharp-shooting contest during the war. He can shoot a pea off a tree stump at two hundred yards."

"My Dad should be here soon, too," Victoria added, catching onto Edward's approach. "He's the captain on the riverboat S.S. *Klondike*."

"I don't think he'll be here any too soon," Red replied. "I saw the *Klondike* paddle wheeler heading up to Dawson City yesterday. Hope you kids aren't telling me tall tales."

"I hope you aren't telling us a tall tale," Charlie threw in.

"Charlie! What's wrong with you?" Victoria scolded. "We have no reason to say such a thing. And yes, you're right about the *Klondike*. It won't be back for a few days. I guess we're nervous being here without our parents."

"Well, my parents are coming back soon," Edward said as he drilled Clara with his eyes to make sure she would keep quiet. There was no way he was going to admit to these men that his mother was in hospital Dawson City and would not be back for weeks.

"Yes," Victoria confirmed. "They could be home tonight." Lying wasn't easy for her, but she had to convince the men that Edward's parents could be back anytime.

"In fact, I thought I saw their boat down river," Clara added in a shaky voice.

"More potatoes?" Victoria asked, feeling like Red could see through their stories as if looking through a clear glass window.

After dinner, the two visitors left for the bunkhouse, not like two friends, but enemies in an uneasy truce.

Charlie offered to bring in an armload of wood, but instead of heading to the wood pile, he crept up to the window of the bunkhouse and peered in. Charlie watched as Red took a package of spaghetti and a can of sauce out of his pack.

Yeah, I knew I was right, Charlie thought. *These thugs stole the food.* Red turned to the window and caught Charlie staring at them.

The big man threw open the door. "What do you think you're up to? I've had enough trouble without having a brat stick his nose into our business!" His angry, bellowing voice carried across the yard over to the big house.

"Nothing," Charlie replied. "Umm," he paused, "just checking to see if you are, well, you know, if you got everything you need. No harm done, right? Now, I best be going."

Victoria heard Red's loud voice and came out on the porch. "Don't you dare yell at my brother! Come here, Charlie. Edward wants us to have a meeting."

"Yeah, kid. Git back to the house before I give you a reason to hightail it," Red scowled.

By this time, Zeke had stepped out of the bunkhouse. "Why are you spying on us? The gold is gone. So is John. My guess is that John has it. End of story."

There's somethin' about that kid dat makes me wonder. I'm gonna keep my eye on him," Red snarled, "and don't let him out of our sight."

Charlie circled over to the woodpile to get an armload of wood and walked slowly back to the big house.

"Let's have a confab in the living room," Edward announced to the other three. "I think each of us should say what we think about these guys...like, are they being straight with us? Is there any danger having them here? What do you think, Victoria?"

"I sure don't like having them around, but I believe Red's story. I am leery of Zeke, though. I would rather die than be in the same room with that creep. He makes me think he's hiding something. I don't think they will hurt us, but I notice that they keep their eyes on us every time we leave the house, as if they're afraid we'll take off."

"They both scare the daylights out of me. I wish Mommy was here." Clara's voice broke, and tears pooled in her eyes.

"We'll never leave you alone with either of those men. You can sleep in my room tonight, Clara," Victoria said, hugging the younger girl.

"What about you, Charlie?" Edward asked. "You've been pretty quiet today."

"I don't know," Charlie replied, looking anxious.

"What's got your tongue?" his sister asked. "This is the first time since you turned four that you don't have an opinion to offer. Something is up with you, so let's hear it."

"We're in this together, kiddo," Edward added. "If any one of us is not willing to work together, there could be problems. I've been uneasy since they arrived. I made sure dad's gun cabinet is locked up, and I've hidden any knives hanging around the kitchen. Might as well be cautious. So, what do you think about the two guys?"

Charlie didn't answer immediately as if he was choosing the right words. "One of them is lying, maybe both."

"And why are you so certain, Detective Sherlock?" Edward questioned.

"Just that I know," Charlie said. "That's all I can say."

"Charlie," Victoria said in a stern voice, "if it turns out you are hiding something I'll tell Father, and you will be in real trouble. Remember, he'll be stopping at Echo Valley on his way back to Whitehorse."

"Let's not make threats, Victoria. I think we should work together and make a plan," Edward advised. "I know you're worried about Charlie, and I am concerned about Clara."

"If you're worried about them, why not use one of Dad's guns and chase them away?" Clara asked.

"Maybe they're armed as well," Edward explained, "and with no adults here to help us, I just can't take the risk. The safest way is for Charlie and Clara to leave. I think you two should secretly take off to Uncle Joe's early tomorrow morning."

"But Edward, that's a long way and we'll be all alone." Clara cuddled closer to Victoria at the thought of travelling through the woods without her older brother or Victoria.

"You know the trail. You've been to Uncle Joe's dozens of times. You'll be safe there. Here's the plan."

The four children sat up for several hours going over the preparations for the next morning.

"Victoria! Get up," Clara nudged her friend. "We slept in. Those men are already in the kitchen, and Charlie and I were supposed to have left by now. What will we do?"

"It's okay," Victoria rubbed her eyes and looked out at the river where the sun glanced across the green water. *Such a gorgeous day. Why couldn't I be reading my book and enjoying myself? It's just not fair!*

Victoria gave Clara a hug. "Carry on with the plan. Charlie will go for an armload of wood, and after he leaves, you go to the outhouse. The two of you will meet up at the woodpile and just slip away. I left two backpacks by the woodpile with sandwiches, dried fruit and a bottle of water for each of you. Charlie added a few more things to his backpack last night—likely more food if I know him—so you should be quite safe and well fed."

Victoria bent to give Clara a little hug. "Now take care on the journey, and be brave. This will all be over as soon as my father returns. He will take these men on the S.S. *Klondike* to Whitehorse, and we'll enjoy our vacation together."

Clara and Charlie were quiet during breakfast, so quiet that Edward and Victoria tried to make casual conversation to keep Red and Zeke from becoming suspicious.

"Charlie," Edward said when he went to the stove for more toast, "how about another armload of wood?"

Charlie was out of his seat in a flash. "Right away, Captain."

Victoria could feel her stomach tighten and those troublesome voices. *He should never be out of my sight. Why am I letting him take off on a long hike to a place I've never been?*

Clara got up from the table and excused herself in a voice that was soft as a whisper.

"And where are you goin'?" Red looked at Clara with an expression that sent shivers through her body.

He'll know I am lying, Clara thought.

"I'm going to the outhouse."

"This is her house, and she can go wherever and whenever she wants." Victoria felt the blood rise in her face. "You are supposed to act like guests, not jail wardens."

"Okay, young lady," Red replied. "Just worried about the young'ns myself. Ain't trying to interfere." He gave her a crooked smile.

Victoria and Edward chatted awkwardly about anything they could think of. Edward talked about the last trapping season and the fall moose hunt. Victoria tried to distract the men by recounting tales of people on the S.S. *Klondike.* A half-hour passed before Red jumped up from the kitchen table.

"Where in tarnation are those kids? How long does it take to git wood, anyway?" He ran for the door and out to the wood pile with Zeke in tow.

"What's going to happen now?" Victoria asked Edward. "What should we do?"

"No matter what happens, they won't find out where Clara and Charlie are headed. Right?"

"For once I totally agree with you." Victoria replied just before Red bounded through the door in a rage.

"Where the blazes are those kids? What's goin' on here? That little brother of yours is up to his ears in trouble. Now, you two tell me exactly where they've gone, or else."

"Or else what?" Victoria said, anger rising in her chest.

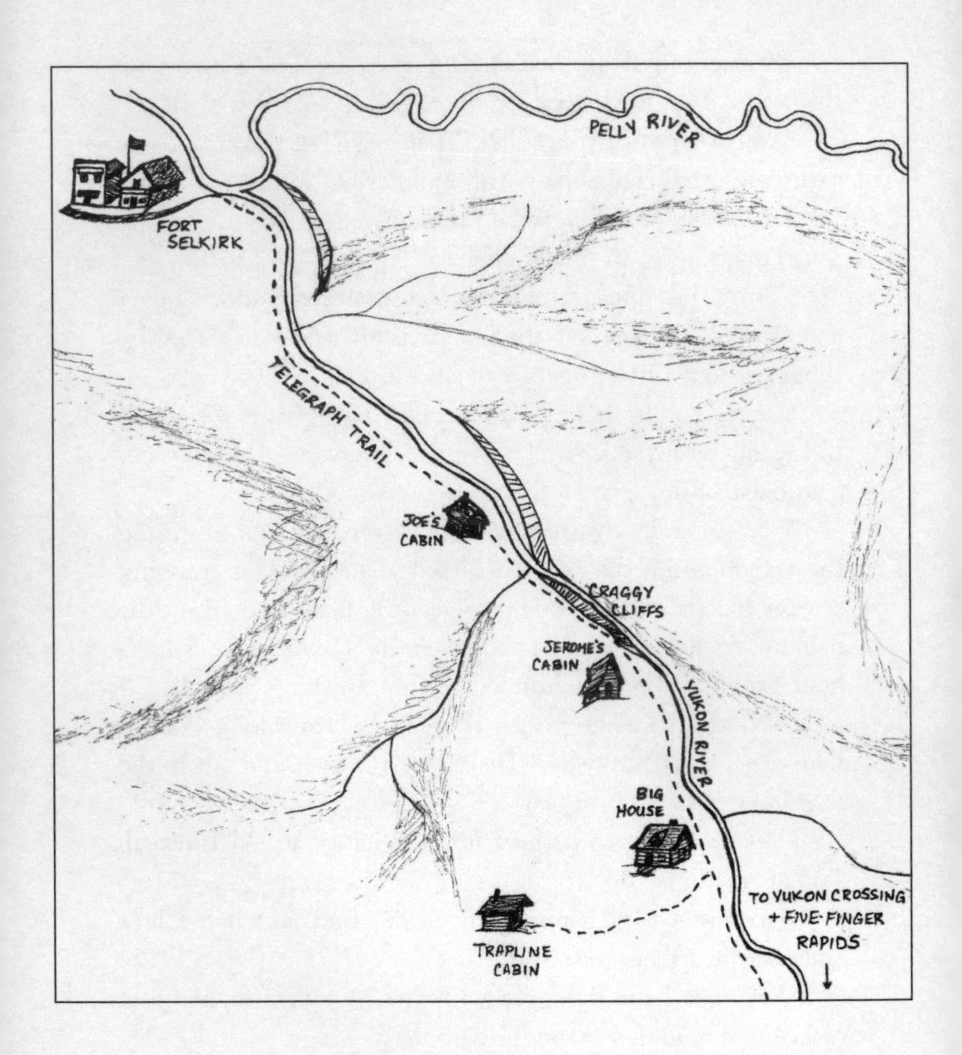
PELLY RIVER
FORT SELKIRK
TELEGRAPH TRAIL
JOE'S CABIN
CRAGGY CLIFFS
JEROME'S CABIN
YUKON RIVER
BIG HOUSE
TO YUKON CROSSING + FIVE-FINGER RAPIDS
TRAPLINE CABIN

"You two are guests here," Edward added. "You will not be telling us what to do, and you certainly will not yell or threaten us."

"When you come storming into the house like that, you can understand why we sent them away. They're just little, and quite honestly, it's better that they left until Mr. and Mrs. McTavish return, which, by the way, could be any time now." Victoria found she had more courage to speak out now that Charlie was safely away from these men.

"I don't like the way you act either," Zeke muttered to Red. "Maybe you're getting crazy from your injured arm. Leave them be. All I want is my gold back."

Edward and Victoria looked at Zeke, puzzled by his unexpected entry into the conversation. At first, Red seemed almost likeable at times, while they were both leery of Zeke. Now they weren't sure.

"We want you to leave now," Edward demanded.

"We ain't goin' nowhere till we find those two kids. And youse are going to find them for us, or else someone is goin' to get hurt." There was no mistaking Red's threat.

Edward and Victoria knew they were dealing with a vicious man, a man who might harm them if he didn't get what he wanted.

Then Edward remembered Charlie's words. *One of them is lying, maybe both.*

Chapter V

Into the Forest

Charlie and Clara dashed along the trail, their backpacks bouncing as they ran as fast as they could to put distance between themselves and the two miners. Clara feared Zeke the most; Charlie mistrusted both men.

"I'm totally pooped," Charlie exclaimed, slowing down to a walk.

"Thanks," Clara replied, out of breath. "My sides are aching, and I can't run another step."

"How much farther to your Uncle's place?"

"It will take most of the day. The trail goes up a couple of hills then down into the valley where Uncle Joe traps."

"What's he like? Old? Young?"

"He's older than our Mom but nothing like her. Uncle Joe finds a joke in everything. You'll like him."

"Will he mind us barging in on him?"

"Not at all. In fact, he jokes that I am such a good seamstress that I should stay with him and make him a moose-skin jacket and a pair of moccasins. He always tells me I'm his favourite niece, then I tell him I am his only niece and we both laugh."

"There won't be anything like corn flakes or hot dogs at his house, so we'll have to eat what he puts on the table. Moose meat for breakfast, lunch and dinner."

"I'm glad Victoria packed us a huge lunch, enough to last until we are back at the big house. Speaking of food, let's stop for a sandwich. I don't think those crooks are going to follow us."

"Why do you call them crooks?" Clara asked, as she took out a sandwich and sat on a log next to where Charlie had set his backpack. She picked up his backpack to move it over. "And what on earth do you have in here? Rocks?"

"Don't touch my pack," Charlie said, grabbing it from Clara.

"You're hiding something, and you'd better tell me what's in there." Clara was not often this determined. "I've never been away from my mom before, and now I'm a mile from home with someone who is keeping secrets."

"I'm not lying to you. I'm just not telling you everything. Sometimes knowing something could be dangerous."

"Not knowing could be dangerous, too," Clara replied. She was suddenly frightened of the bush, tired from the exhausting trip and desperately missing her mother. She just wanted to be back at the big house, helping her mother sew and cook. She wasn't old enough to be on her own with a boy who was keeping a secret, maybe a dangerous secret. Clara felt like crying but held back. Instead, she stuffed the remainder of the sandwich in her mouth and plodded down the trail, not even looking to see if Charlie was following.

"Hey! Wait up for me!" Charlie hollered. "Please don't be mad at me! If we make it to your uncle's, I'll tell you everything!" Clara stopped, and Charlie continued in a kind voice. "You see, Clara, it's this way. One of those guys is really bad, but I don't know which one. If they catch us, it's better if you don't know what I know."

"You aren't making any sense. But anyway, I am not really mad at you. I'm just tired and worried. I want to get to Uncle Joe's place where it's safe."

She started down the path with Charlie a few steps behind.

The mood at the big house was tense. "You better tell us where those brats have gone. I don't want anyone leaving while we're here. You git that?" Red glared at them, looking as mean as a wolverine.

"Look, mister," Edward said. "We've bandaged your arm. We've given you food and a bed to sleep in. We've had about enough of being bullied around in our own house. My parents will be back, and my Dad will put you straight, so better not push us around. I'll tell you what. Take our small boat to Fort Selkirk and wait there until the *Klondike* arrives. It should be there in a few days."

"That's the best for everyone. There's a policeman in Fort Selkirk, and you can tell him about the robbery," Victoria added.

"Maybe best to leave 'em here and git ourselves to Fort Selkirk," Zeke muttered in an uncertain voice, a rat-like expression on his face. "But as far as cops go, we don't never talk to cops."

"Don't be stupid, Zeke, we ain't leaving these two!" Red yelled. "We're all stickin' together until we find Charlie! Youse two will do exactly as I say, or the little miss will be in trouble. We gotta find those kids, and you're gonna help us or I'll git Zeke to tie Goldilocks to the chair and then see if the hero here is going to be as brassy."

"You lowlife crooks stay clear of Victoria!" Edward yelled. "What do you want from us that we haven't already given you? What are you up to?"

"We just want to ask Charlie some questions. Tell us where they are, and no one'll git hurt. I know you can see that Zeke is dangerous. You don't want to deal with someone like him. He may have killed John, for all I know. No one seed his body. I think Zeke did him in and took the gold. Then again, maybe Victoria's smartass little brother took the gold."

Victoria and Edward looked at each other, both realizing that they should never have befriended these strangers, and both trying to think of some way to escape from what could be their worst nightmare.

"I think we'd better tell them, Victoria."

"Yes, let's tell the truth so there's no more trouble."

"They've gone up to the trapline cabin," Edward said.

"Is that the truth? What does Goldilocks say?"

"Yes, they're hiking to the trapline cabin where they'll be safe," Victoria answered, her voice quavering.

"Well, I say that you two are lying. We can check the trail for their footprints, so stop fibbing. Now I will just git Zeke to take the little miss there and tie her up until I git the truth."

"All right! They've taken the Telegraph Trail to the police station at Fort Selkirk," Edward said nervously.

"Nah. I don't buy that neither. You wouldn't expect two little ones to walk twenty miles, so I figures they're going somewheres closer. Their footprints are on the trail north to Fort Selkirk but they ain't goin' that far, so where are they headin'?"

"I don't care what you do. I am not telling you," Victoria said defiantly.

"Youse are going to help me find 'em, so pack some grub, put on your hiking boots and let's catch those kids. When we find 'em, we won't touch a hair on their heads, but if you fool around with me anymore, I won't be responsible for what Zeke might do to the little missy here." A wicked smile crossed his face, now even more threatening. "Now, git ready."

Edward and Victoria stuffed beef jerky, dried fruit and bread in a pack, along with jars of water and a couple of jackets. Red and Zeke were picking up their gear from the bunkhouse.

"Okay, let's go," Red demanded, taking the trail heading north. "Double time!" he yelled, leading off with long strides. Even Zeke had trouble keeping up to the tall, hefty man.

"Come on, missy, don't pretend you can't run. Move it!" Red shouted when Victoria dropped behind, purposely trying to slow them down.

"Watch what you say to her!" Edward yelled, trying to control his urge to punch the burly man's face.

"So, you want to act like a big man, do you? Well, take this!" Red jabbed a fist into Edward's chest. The tall, slim boy staggered back, boiling with anger.

"I'll flatten your ugly face!" Edward yelled, raising his fists at the bulky miner.

"Edward! Stop! Don't fight him. You'll just make matters worse. At least now we know we are dealing with dirty low-down crooks and maybe even murderers."

"I didn't murder John, but I have my suspicions," Zeke muttered.

"You're more of a crook than me," Red fumed. "You probably have the gold and let that little rascal steal it from you."

"Maybe John didn't run off like you said. Maybe you made certain he couldn't run," Zeke mumbled.

"Shut your trap, Zeke! You want to git a bullet in your head?" Red yelled.

"You're both a couple of lying crooks! It is hard to tell who is telling the biggest whoppers," Edward blurted out. "And to think I actually defended the two of you because I believed your partner really had robbed you. My parents will see you in jail for the rest of your useless lives. You'll see."

"You'll never see them again if you don't move faster and find those brats. Now git goin', both of you." Red pushed Edward down the trail and turned back to Victoria. "And missy, how about you callin' out for your brother every few minutes. He will come if you say so."

"He comes when I whistle." She began to whistle an SOS. She whistled one long, one short, one long. It was the signal for Charlie to hide. The sound was clear and loud. It echoed through the forest and bounced against the valley slopes.

If only he can hear me, she thought.

Charlie and Clara were on the Telegraph Trail, not far ahead of their pursuers.

"Listen!" Charlie whispered. "Can you hear that?"

Clara stopped on the trail. A long blast, one short, then another long one.

"It's Victoria," Clara said with relief. "She wants us to turn back to the big house."

"No! Be quiet! She wants us to hide. Quick! Follow me."

Charlie grabbed Clara's wrist and led her off the trail into the thick bush.

"Don't make a sound." Charlie was tense.

"What's up with you? Are you crazy or something?" Clara tried to pull away and return to the trail. Charlie tightened his grip on her wrist.

"Please, Clara, we're in danger," he whispered. "When Victoria whistles an SOS, it means there is trouble and we must hide. You have to listen to me."

"Okay, but I really wish I could be back with my brother and Victoria. I hate it out here in the bush, and I don't know if you're much help."

"Shush." Charlie pulled Clara farther into the woods. She glanced back for a final look at the Telegraph Trail and caught a glimpse of Red and Zeke and then saw the worried look on Victoria's face. Clara was relieved that she had followed Charlie into hiding.

Yes, something is terribly wrong. This isn't part of the plan.

They continued farther into the bush, being careful not to make a sound until they were well back from the trail.

The two children crouched down, concealed in the dense underbrush. Mosquitoes swarmed about them, landing and feeding on their blood. They were afraid to slap at the bugs since even the slightest noise might be heard by the thugs that were searching for them.

"Why didn't my sister put some bug dope in my pack?" Charlie whispered. Clara could see an army of mosquitoes perched on Charlie's neck like a pack of pigs at a trough. When she brushed the bloodsucking pests from his neck, her hand came away streaked with blood. They seemed to like Charlie's light complexion more than her own dark skin. The longer the children remained motionless, the more vicious the bugs became. Now they were driving Clara crazy as well. The mosquitoes seemed to sense the children were defenceless victims.

We're fresh meat to them, she thought, waving her hand at the swarm.

"These bugs are too much! I can't sit still any longer." Charlie muttered. "Let's move farther from the trail, but quietly. I don't know which is worse, being eaten alive by mosquitoes or having those crooks catch us. If we can keep moving, I won't become a meal for a million bugs."

They crept through the woods until they reached a small gully choked with willows. They pushed their way through the aspen growth and discovered a stream trickling out of a beaver dam. The bushes and trees were so thick, the children were hidden from all directions.

"Cool water!" Charlie stooped to drink.

"Don't drink from streams like this! Don't you see the beaver dam upriver? You could get sick."

"It's not like in the big cities where they put oil and garbage into the rivers and lakes." He took a long drink and washed his itchy bites with the icy water.

Clara washed her face and cooled the angry mosquito bites by splashing water on her neck, then reached in her pack for her water bottle and drank. The water was warm and did little to refresh her.

"Haven't you ever learned about giardia?" Clara asked. "It's a stomach disease that you get if there are animals near the water like muskrats or beavers."

"Beaver fever! Sure, but I didn't think we had to worry about anything way out here. Anyway, I just took one drink."

"You're funny. You save us from the bad guys and then risk getting giardia because you don't understand that beavers poop in the streams, and the water could make you awfully sick."

"I guess I'll try and study when I go back to school next fall. Maybe there is something useful in schoolbooks after all. Now, I think we should get trucking, as your big brother would say. Do you think we could head back to the Telegraph Trail but travel through the woods for a while to make sure those crooks don't see us?"

They both turned in different directions.

"The trail's over there, isn't it?" Clara said, pointing to the north.

"I thought we came from there," Charlie said, pointing east, "but maybe you're right. Gee, it's confusing when you get off the trail and can't see anything but bush and trees. You lead the way because you seem pretty certain." Charlie picked up his pack and followed Clara. "Let's find the trail but stay out of sight in the bush."

They walked for half an hour in the direction Clara thought would lead them to the trail.

"I wish we could at least get back to the Telegraph Trail. I agree with you that we should stay in the bush but keep the trail in sight. I sure don't want to get lost out here." As Clara said these words she had the uncomfortable feeling that they may already be lost.

"We should be back on the Telegraph Trail by now," Charlie said. "Maybe I was right, and it was the other direction. Let's stop and think about this for a minute. I'm hungry anyway. Maybe some food will get my brain cells working."

"Okay," Clara said, "We ran off the trail to our left. That would be towards the mountains, not towards the Yukon River. Too bad we didn't go off towards the river. My uncle's cabin is next to the river. We'd just have to follow along the bank going downstream, and we'd find his house. Do you remember where the sun was when we were on the trail?"

"It was behind us," Charlie answered, "but that was around noon."

"What time is it now?" Clara asked.

Charlie rolled up his sleeve and looked at his wrist. "Two freckles past skin o'clock," he said with a grin.

"What?"

"Just a joke. I forgot my watch, and I don't know what time it is for sure. I think we left the trail about two hours ago. It could be about two o'clock, and the sun should still be in the south."

"My uncle's place is north of our house," Clara said.

"The sun sets in the east, so we should head west to find the Telegraph Trail," Charlie suggested.

"Don't be a dodo. The sun sets in the west, so we have to go east to get to the Telegraph Trail but not straight east. At this time of year, the sun sets a bit to the northwest because of the inclination of the earth's axis in August."

"Boy, you're pretty smart, and you don't even go to school," Charlie said with admiration.

Clara did not hear that as a compliment and was upset that Charlie seemed to think she was a country bumpkin. "Of course, I go to school. We take home school. There's nothing to do in the winter but study, so I get all A's, and sometimes I study Edward's textbooks as well. That's how I know about the solar system."

"But I was right about which direction we should go, without knowing all that book stuff," Charlie said, feeling embarrassed at having this girl from the wood camp teach him his lessons.

"We must have gone west when we left the Telegraph Trail. So, let's go directly east, and we should get back to the trail. Are you okay with that?" Clara asked. They checked their bearings and headed off. They hiked for another hour crouching down to get through thick clusters of willows and crawling over fallen logs.

"My mom never lets me go into the bush alone, not even a little way, so I'm not very good at finding my way. Ouch!" Clara let out a cry as a sharp branch jabbed her. She felt her arm and pulled away blood-stained fingers .

"Let's see," Charlie pulled back the torn shirt. A nasty scrape was bleeding, but the cut wasn't deep. "Victoria packed some bandages for us. My sister was her usual cautious, worrying type, so I can patch up your arm."

Clara was relieved to sit on a log while Charlie applied a piece of soft gauze.

"There," he said. "It will feel better in a minute."

"Thanks, Charlie. Maybe you won't like this, but right now, you sound just like your sister," Clara said with a laugh.

"This may surprise you, but I would do anything to hear my sister give one whistle blast and see her waiting for me on the trail, especially if she could put something on my bug bites to stop them from itching and then make me a whopper of a hamburger for supper."

"We still have two sandwiches left. We'll be okay as long as we get to Uncle Joe's tonight." Again, Clara's secret voice told her they were not going to be out of the woods for supper, maybe not even tomorrow or the day after.

Charlie noticed her worried look. "What's wrong, Clara?"

"We are really lost, aren't we? Some kids get lost, and they're never found alive. I think we're that kind of lost." Clara turned her head away so that Charlie wouldn't see the tears in her eyes.

"We'll find the trail or the Yukon River. We just need to get up higher where we can see the mountains or maybe even the river. We have to keep a stiff upper lip as my dad would say. I feel pretty bad at times, and then I tell myself to smarten up because moping will not get us anywhere. All of a sudden, we'll stumble out on the trail, or we'll find a stream that will lead us to the river. Let's not panic. We'll make it. We'll just keep walking east."

"At least we're together. Wouldn't it be frightening to be out here alone, especially if you have to spend the night out here? Are we going to have to sleep in the woods tonight, Charlie? It's getting dark, and I feel so tired I could curl up and drop to sleep in a second."

"Let's look for some shelter, some place where the bugs won't carry us off as soon as we close our eyes."

As Charlie and Clara searched for shelter, Edward and Victoria continued on their way to Fort Selkirk with Red and Zeke urging them forward.

"Them kids must have travelled faster 'n lightning. Where did you tell 'em to go?" The big man's voice was threatening.

"As I said," Edward replied, "they've gone to get the cops."

"If youse are telling the truth this time, we'll make sure they never deliver the message. We're going back to get that motorboat, and you young'ns are going to take us upstream to Fort Selkirk. We will stop at every cabin on the Yukon River from here to Fort Selkirk until we find them brats. Now, let's go. It's late, and we gotta be back at the house and on our way downstream at daybreak."

"They aren't brats. Now I know that you two are just a couple of crooks. You probably killed your partner and plan to kill us, too!" Edward yelled.

A wavering, uncertain declaration came from Zeke. "It's like Red said, John made off with our gold."

"We don't trust either of you, and when we get back to the house, my dad will be there, so you'd better watch out."

"I heard that one before. What I thinks is that your parents went to Dawson City, and they ain't coming back to help you out. So, watch out, Mister Big Talk, or your little girlfriend might be in trouble," Red growled. "Now, let's make tracks."

Red and Zeke led the way back to the big house. Edward and Victoria followed silently, mulling Red's story over in their minds. Neither could quite decide if he was lying, if Zeke was or if they both were.

That night, Victoria locked her door and lodged a chair against the handle. She slept fitfully, troubled by nightmares:

Zeke placing a gun to her head; Charlie being chased by a grizzly; Edward fighting the burly miner and ending up in a pool of blood on the kitchen floor. She woke with a start, her heart pounding, and before trying to get back to sleep, she prayed that Charlie and Clara were sleeping safely at Uncle Joe's.

Chapter VI

Overnight in the Forest

Charlie and Clara struggled through the thick woods for another hour until they came to a large fir tree with branches that swept down to the ground, creating a circular shelter.

"How about this for our home away from home?" Charlie asked, attempting to dispel dark thoughts of the oncoming night. They could no longer see the sun, but the western horizon was streaked with pink and golden rays.

Clara pushed aside the long fir branches, crawled into the shelter and collapsed on the ground.

"You need something to sleep on," Charlie said, breaking off a few fir branches and pushing them into the shelter. "Make a mattress with these, and I will give you some more branches to cover yourself. Even if it's a warm night, we'll need protection from the bugs, and if it's cold, we need the branches to keep us from freezing our tootsies."

Clara arranged a carpet of branches and curled up again, pulling several of the sweet-smelling boughs over her. She rested her head on the fir boughs and immediately fell asleep.

Charlie squirmed about for a few minutes, found a comfortable spot on the branches, and using his pack as a pillow, dropped off to sleep.

"Ouch!" Charlie yelled. "I'm being eaten alive!"

"What?" Clara woke to see her companion slapping madly at his neck. "Just mosquitoes, and do they ever like the taste of you. Your face looks like a pin cushion."

"They feasted on me all night! I could hardly sleep!"

"I slept like a log. No bad dreams, just dead to the world. It must be late because the sun is already high up in the sky. We'll find the trail today. I just feel it." Clara crawled out of their shelter and looked around, hoping the trail would miraculously appear a few steps away.

They breakfasted on dried fruit and lukewarm water, then whacked their way through the heavy underbrush, using the position of the sun to maintain an easterly direction.

The day was cool with a threat of rain. All sense of optimism disappeared as the day wore on. "What if the sun disappears?" Clara said in a worried voice. "We won't know which way to go."

"Let's take our bearings right now so that if it really clouds over, we'll still be on course."

"Nothing looks familiar." Clara felt discouraged and then had the sinking, worrisome thought that they would never find their way out of the forest.

"If we lose the sun, we'll have to think of another way. Right now, I am too tired and hungry to think. Do you want to stop for a snack?"

"We only have one sandwich left," Clara said rummaging through her pack. "Maybe we should only have one bite each so we don't run out of food." The little worried voice told her they would be out of food tomorrow and the next day, and that they would either die of starvation or be supper for a hungry grizzly as desperate for food as the two lost children.

"Don't be a worrywart," Charlie said. "Every once in a while, you get a doomed look on your face as if you've given up. What you have to do is tell yourself we're going to be okay. Promise me?"

"We'll be okay," Clara repeated with little conviction. "Edward will find us, or your sister will send out a search party of thousands and tear the woods apart until she finds us."

Back at the big house, Victoria was awakened by loud voices. She snuck down the hallway and knocked on Edward's door. They went downstairs together and found Red and Zeke looking through the kitchen cupboards.

"Throw some grub in a sack, and then write a note for your parents explaining that everything is just hunky-dory and all of you went to Fort Selkirk to buy groceries. We don't want your parents sending out the Mounties when they find you missing. Get some paper and a pencil, and I'll tell youse exactly what to write."

Victoria hesitated, realizing that her only hope for rescue was that her father would arrive at Echo Valley and put these men in their place, and that place would be the nearest jail or, more likely, the hangman's noose.

"Git on with it, girl!" Red yelled. "Let me see the note, and no tricks either."

"You'd better do as he says," Edward said. "We have enough trouble without getting him any angrier. Maybe he is just acting like a thug because he lost the gold. Then again, maybe he is a thug and may hurt us."

"You got that right, kid," Red said to Edward. "I never hurt young'ns, but if I git anymore trouble from youse, I just may change my mind. Now go down, and git a boat ready. Those kids got to be somewhere between here and the fort, and I have something I need to ask Charlie."

It was two hours before Edward returned from the dock. "We have to take the river canoe and use the small outboard. It's only a four-horse power and will be pretty slow. My dad has the big motor apart, and I wasn't able to fix it."

"We'll take whatever will get us to Fort Selkirk. Come on, girl!" Red yelled at Victoria, who was feeding the chickens and dogs, and making sure Sheba and her pups were comfortable. She was purposely carrying out each chore slowly. Each hour Edward and Victoria delayed the departure gave their younger siblings additional time to get free from the clutches of these dangerous men.

It was late afternoon when they walked down to the dock and loaded the canoe. It was lighter than the motorboat, but they could either paddle or power it with a motor, and it was big enough to carry four people. Red and Zeke sat in the middle, Edward piloted the boat and Victoria sat in the bow.

She worried about Charlie. For the first time since their mother died, Charlie was away from his big sister's protection. Victoria imagined the many dangers the two children may be facing. The grizzly from her dream was stalking Charlie, and she imagined Clara tripping and falling into the fast-flowing Yukon River.

When she looked at Red with his angry scowl and at Zeke with his shifty eyes, she felt some relief that, at least, Charlie was safe from these men. But that wouldn't be for long. Red and Zeke intended to make them stop at all the cabins along the river. Unless Uncle Joe was watching the children every minute, Charlie and Clara could fall into their clutches. Then she thought of a way to escape.

"Edward, I was just thinking about Buster's Roll and thought we should put it to use on this trip. What do you think?"

"That's a good idea. Those techniques would work quite well with this canoe," Edward replied, catching Victoria's wink. "When?"

"Right now."

Edward banked the boat sharply, and he and Victoria threw their weight against the gunnels. The boat overturned, throwing all four of them into the water. Victoria and Edward were ready for the icy plunge and grabbed hold of the overturned boat. Red and Zeke were swept downstream by the powerful river current. Zeke struggled in the water, yelling for Red to save him.

"Quick. Get under, and let's turn it right side up!" Edward yelled.

The two teenagers ducked and came up under the boat, able to breathe and see one another in the space created by the hull. They had to rock the boat until they broke the vacuum that pasted the gunnels to the water.

"One, two, three. NOW!" Edward yelled, and both teens pushed up with all their strength on one side of the canoe.

The boat righted itself, with Edward and Victoria clinging to the sides. Edward slithered into the boat and steadied it so Victoria could climb in.

"Wow! We made it, and look, Red is still trying to drag Zeke to shore. Goodbye and good riddance to you!" Victoria yelled. "Now let's get to your Uncle's place and find Charlie and Clara. I am worried sick about them."

Edward pulled the chain to start the motor. It only sputtered. He tinkered with the motor as the two miners struggled to make it to shore. Victoria wondered why Red was rescuing Zeke, and then it came to her that the location of the gold was still a mystery, and that Zeke might have taken it. Red would not risk letting the answer to the location of the gold sink into the Yukon River along with Zeke. She watched as Zeke stood up in the waist-high water and staggered to shore. Red saw that the two teens were having trouble with the motor.

"I don't know if it will go, Victoria. I'll have to take a look at the carb to see if it took on water."

"Hurry Edward, or Red will try to swim out to us."

"It's better to do everything slowly and carefully when it comes to motors. If you hurry," he said as he removed the casing, "it will just take longer. Could you hold these screws while I get the water out of the carburetor?"

Once Victoria began to help, her anxiety lessened. In a few minutes, Edward had the engine back together.

"Now, let's hope it starts."

"Bless you, little engine," Victoria whispered. Before she got the words out of her mouth, she spotted Red swimming towards them. Her stomach was in knots as she watched him take strong strokes, closing the distance between him and the boat.

Edward pulled on the chain to start the motor. The engine sputtered and died. In two more strokes, Red would be close enough to grab onto the boat. Edward tried again, and the motor caught.

"We're on our way!" Victoria yelled. "Goodbye to the rubbish in the river!" she yelled as the boat putted away from Red. The angry man cursed and swam back to shore.

Edward pointed the boat downstream, heading for his uncle's cabin.

"Soon we'll all be together again, and everything will be great," Victoria said.

"Tomorrow, we could make supper at the big house," Edward continued, "and in a few days, your dad should be back with a load of groceries, and we can get him to send the police after those guys."

"If only," Victoria repeated. These words sent her back to worrying again. *If only Charlie and Clara are safe at Uncle Joe's. They* have *to be there.*

Rain pelted down, and dark clouds hung over the river. Edward and Victoria shivered in their wet clothing as the boat made its way downstream aided by the strong current. The thought of seeing Charlie and Clara again kept their spirits up, despite the miserable rain. Then suddenly, the engine sputtered and died.

"Water in the engine," muttered Edward. "Gotta go on shore to fix it this time. I have to be certain it will get us all the way to Uncle Joe's."

They both grabbed paddles and turned the boat to shore, landing near an opening in the forest that led to the base of steep cliffs. "It's turning miserable, and I'm soaked. I guess you don't have any dry matches on you, do you?" Victoria asked, shivering with cold.

Charlie and Clara plodded along, feeling the grip of hunger, yet not wanting to eat the last of their food. The sun disappeared behind the clouds, and the two weren't sure if it was night or if it was just a dark, cloudy day. Once again, they searched for a shelter, this time looking for something that would protect them from the rain.

"There's no place to sleep, and I'm too tired to continue," Clara muttered, barely able to move one foot in front of the other. "Maybe we should just lie down here and sleep, and then go on in an hour or so."

"We need some cover. It's going to rain, and it's already getting dark. Better to keep going until we find a dry place. We need to have a shelter, otherwise we'll be too tired to get anywhere tomorrow."

"Make us a shelter like my Uncle Joe makes. I'm too tired, but I'll tell you how he makes a cozy place to sleep." Charlie put down his pack and went to work while Clara gave instructions for the lean-to.

First, he gathered up several small logs that he leaned against a huge fallen tree.

"Once you have all the logs in place, break off lots of spruce branches and cover the logs with several layers," Clara told him as she rested against a tree trunk.

"I'm glad your uncle taught you bushcraft, and I bet you're pleased that I'm such a top-notch house builder." Charlie smiled as he inspected his completed project. "Not all that bad." Despite the onset of their second night in the woods, he tried to be cheerful and hide his anxiety over the cold, uncomfortable night ahead and the coming storm.

"Hey girl, don't go to sleep out here. Up with you, right now! It's starting to rain, and you'll get soaked." Clara moaned and rolled over. Charlie tugged on her sleeve. "Hey, time for bed, and not out here in the rain. You know what farmers say about their dumb chickens—not enough brains to get out of the rain."

That brought Clara to her feet. Charlie led the way to the makeshift shelter as lightning lit the sky and the first of the rain pelted at them. "That's better. Now, have a good sleep."

She tried to find a comfortable spot on the fir branches, but it wasn't a good sleep for Charlie or Clara. The rain came down in sheets and seeped into the primitive shelter.

Chapter VII

The Lost Children

As Charlie and Clara slept fitfully through the cold, wet, northern night, Edward and Victoria were on shore taking the engine apart.

"Oh, rats!" Edward exclaimed. "Am I dumb!"

"What's the matter?" Victoria sat crouching on a log, shivering, her arms wrapped about her chest.

"I forgot to fill the gas tank!"

"Well, I'll be!" Victoria laughed. "I was beginning to think you never made mistakes. You're human after all."

"It's not funny. Do you realize we will have to walk to Uncle Joe's? And to get there, we have to scale the cliffs, something I have no intention of doing in the dark, with the rain pelting down the rocks."

"So, we're sleeping here until daylight? Well, I'm not freezing to death in the rain. Come on. Let's find some shelter." Victoria scampered up, running through a clearing over to the edge of the cliffs. "I bet there's a dry space under that rock overhang."

Edward pulled the boat up onto the gravel bar and followed Victoria. He had a bag of food that had been tied to the boat gunnels. "I should have put some dry clothes in a waterproof bag," Edward said. "My second mistake, and this one will cost us. You're already cold."

"I warmed up a little running over here, and the food will help. Let's get under the cliff and see what food tastes like when it's been dunked in the Yukon River." There was just enough room for them to sit out of the rain.

Victoria rummaged through the bag, tossing out the wet biscuits. "Do you realize that if you're shivering from cold, food will actually warm you up? It's just like your body becomes a furnace, and the food is firewood."

"Well, pass me some firewood, girl."

"Raisins, beef jerky and cheese! Yum. Here. There's lots, and all washed clean."

Victoria divided the food, and when they finished, Victoria leaned her head on Edward's shoulder. Soon they were both asleep.

"Wake up," Edward whispered. "We gotta get moving. It's still raining, but at least there's enough light for us to climb."

"Ouch, my neck is stiff." She crawled out from under the rock overhang and looked up at the cliffs. "No problem. I like rock climbing."

"That's good. You lead because I'm afraid of heights," Edward admitted.

"Another chink in your armor!" Victoria smiled. "The first few days at Echo Valley, I thought you could do everything. Now I discover you make mistakes and that you are actually afraid of something. Hallelujah! Okay, if we are going to climb this wall, we need a couple of ropes from the boat. Can you fetch them?"

Edward was off like a shot, and in minutes, he returned with the ropes.

"I'll start climbing and then let the rope down for you. If you're afraid of heights, don't look down. Just look for the next handhold."

The rain continued to drizzle down as Victoria began scaling the cliff. At first it was easy because there were tiny spruce trees and willows growing in the crevices. When she reached the last of the trees, she tied the rope onto a small spruce tree growing out of a crevice. Victoria made certain the knot was secure before throwing the other half of the rope down to Edward.

"My knots can hold an ox. You can put all your weight on the rope and climb."

Edward moved cautiously up the cliff, placing his hands and feet carefully before taking the next step. Soon he reached Victoria.

"Hold onto the tree and stay here while I climb to the top." Victoria scampered up the rock face as nimble and sure as a spider.

"I'm at the top!" She secured the rope around a boulder and threw the end down to Edward.

"Yikes! I hate this!" Edward muttered, as he took his first tentative steps up the steepest section of the rock face.

"You won't fall as long as you have a firm grip on the rope. I tied a couple of knots on the rope to give you something to grab onto. You'll be fine."

Edward gritted his teeth and started the climb, wishing he was anywhere but on this steep pitch where a misstep would send him tumbling down a hundred feet onto a pile of rocks.

"You made it!" Victoria said, reaching her hand out to Edward as he struggled up the final few feet. "Now we just have to get down the other side of the cliffs. Hey! It's beautiful up here! And look, there's a cabin. Someone lives just over there."

"That is someone you do not want to meet," Edward said, as he plunked himself down on the safe, flat surface at the top. "Crazy Jerome lives there, and we locals have nothing to do with him."

"I'll take your word for that. In any case, I want to get to Uncle Joe's as fast as we can to see Charlie and Clara again."

"I'll show you how to get down." Victoria secured the rope around a sturdy boulder, making sure the knots were tight. She swung herself over the edge, and holding the rope, she rappelled down the steep cliff.

"Okay, Edward, your turn. Keep your legs straight out and just walk backwards down the cliff."

"It may be simple for you, but this scares the living daylights out of me." He grabbed the rope and started backing down the cliff. The rocks were wet and slippery, and his feet slipped out from him. He dangled above the drop, clinging desperately to the rope. "Yikes! Are you trying to kill me?"

"You're okay, as long as you don't let go of the rope," she said calmly. "Now, I want you to put your legs out straight onto the rock face and let your body swing out perpendicular to the pitch, otherwise the rappel doesn't work."

Grimly, he obeyed her, holding onto her words as firmly as he was gripping the rope.

"Holy smokes!" Edward gasped as he touched the ground. "Am I glad to get to the bottom! And look, there's the Telegraph Trail. We'll be at Uncle Joe's in an hour."

And indeed, it was not long before the two teenagers spotted the log cabin.

"There it is!" Edward announced cheerfully. "Just in time for breakfast with Uncle Joe."

"And hopefully Charlie and Clara!"

Victoria ran ahead, anxious to find her brother. She was about to rush through the door when it occurred to her that Uncle Joe didn't know her from a hole in the wall, an expression her little brother liked to use.

She waited for Edward, her heart racing. *They have to be here, safe and well looked after. I will never forgive myself if anything has happened to Charlie.*

Edward opened the door a crack. "Uncle? It's Edward."

There was a muffled reply from inside the cabin. "Come on in. I'm about to put the coffee pot on."

"Are Clara and Charlie here?" Victoria asked, without waiting until they were in the house.

"Who's that?" Uncle Joe asked. "Sounds like a strange woman, so hold on there until I get my pants on. Clara's at the big house as far as I know."

Victoria's heart felt like it weighed a ton. *If Clara wasn't here, then Charlie must be missing as well. Where are they?*

Victoria was swept with panic, and her stomach tightened into a knot.

"Take it easy, Victoria. We don't know for sure yet. Let's talk to Uncle. He'll help."

"The coast is clear."

It was dark inside the log cabin. Victoria's eyes adjusted to the dim light. Smiling at her was a muscular and fit Indigenous man with a twinkle in his eyes.

"And is this your young wife?" Uncle Joe asked with a grin.

"I'm Victoria," she answered in a serious tone. "Please tell me that you've seen Charlie and Clara."

"Now, who in tarnation is Charlie? Oh, I get it! You're Captain Russell's cubs. Well, I haven't seen Charlie, and I haven't seen little Clara, at least not since I visited the big house a month ago. Now, tell me what's going on. "

Edward recounted the entire story from the time his mother was injured.

"Sure seems like you fell in with a couple of lowlife crooks. Now let's see, the two young ones have been missing for two nights, and they were headed for my cabin as far as you know. Do you think they lost their way between the big house and here?"

"They're lost. I am certain of it," Victoria spoke in a voice sounding of utter despair.

"Now don't get on like that, young woman. We'll find 'em."

"Uncle Joe knows these woods better than the woodpeckers, the wolverines and the grizzlies all put together, and his dog Bruiser can follow a trail for days."

"Not grizzlies!" Victoria cried. "Are there grizzlies? Could the children have been attacked and eaten?!"

"I understand why you are so upset, being that you're responsible for your brother. We'll find them. Let's pack some supplies. We'll take Bruiser to help us track, and we'll pick up their trail in no time. If I can follow a moose for a week, I sure can follow a couple of young ones who leave behind broken twigs, candy wrappers, orange peels and footprints."

"Uncle is one of the best trackers in the Yukon. Whenever one of those chechakos is lost or the Mounties need a criminal tracked, they ask Uncle to help. He has never failed."

"And I won't fail when it's my little niece out there in the middle of the forest without food for days. We need a tarp, bandages, matches, warm clothing and lots of food," he said as he moved quickly around the cabin, stuffing supplies into three backpacks.

By the time they left the cabin, it was mid-morning. Clouds still obscured the sun.

"Once we leave the Telegraph Trail, how can you tell which way to go if there is no sun?" Victoria asked, not quite believing that this man from the backwoods could track children who had a two-day head start.

"Uncle could be blindfolded, and he would still know which way is north or south, so don't waste your energy worrying, Victoria. Think of where they may have left the trail. Where were we when you warned Charlie to hide? That is where Uncle will start searching for signs."

"Signs? Signs of what?" *They would never find the children. If Uncle Joe led them into the woods, they would all be lost... all five of them!* Victoria felt sick with worry as they started along the Telegraph Trail.

Uncle Joe did not take his eyes off the ground. Bruiser ran ahead sniffing the bushes and running along the game trails. Occasionally, the dog took off chasing a squirrel.

"They haven't come this way," Uncle Joe announced after they had been on the trail for an hour. Victoria tried to remember what the trail looked like when she whistled a warning to Charlie.

She calmed her mind and visualized the trail. *Is there anything different that would help me remember that part of the trail? It was all the same bush and the same type of trees.* They continued down the trail for another hour until Uncle Joe motioned them to stop.

"Now, I see several footsteps. Look. There's your footprint," Uncle Joe said to Edward, "and yours, young woman. And look! There's a print for a big man and one of slight build. These footsteps go both ways. So, this is where you turned back. Is that right?"

"I remember we turned around about an hour after Victoria whistled a warning to Charlie."

"Trees and bushes, trees and bushes, and they all look the same," Victoria said, wanting so very much to be able to help the tracker pick up the children's trail but feeling helpless.

"Nothing looks the same. Footsteps are different. I see when you were running and when you became tired and slowed down. I see where the big guy stopped, maybe he was telling you to pick up the pace."

"You're right. How can you know that?" For the first time, she felt a glimmer of hope.

"Always look carefully at where you are going and where you are coming from. Notice the small things in the bush—the gnarled tree, the old stump, the woodpecker's home and the midden where the squirrels leave their leftovers after eating spruce cones."

They walked for almost an hour before Uncle Joe stopped once again to study the ground. "I would know that little shoeprint anywhere. And come look here, this must be your brother's footprint. See, they stopped and then took off into the bush. Too bad they went left into the trees. If they had gone to the other side of the trail, they would have headed for the river, and Clara could have led them to my cabin, trail or no trail. We'll find them, though, as long as they leave us signs."

Uncle Joe led the way through the forest, stopping every few minutes to inspect a broken branch and place his hand on a footprint that he could see but was invisible to Edward and Victoria. Bruiser ran ahead picking up the scent. Every few minutes, Victoria blew on the whistle a long single blast, the signal for Charlie to come. Hours passed. Uncle Joe and Bruiser never lost the trail, but neither did they catch up to the lost children.

As the day wore on, dark clouds moved across the sky, and the rain began first in a drizzle and then a downpour. Uncle Joe seemed unaffected by the rain. However, as it grew darker, it took him longer to track footsteps and signs of the children. Victoria was visibly tired, and Edward was slowing down.

Chapter VIII

Hurtful Words in the Woods

Clara and Charlie awoke to thunder and lightning, shivered and fell again into a fitful sleep, only to be awakened later by the roar of thunder and the rain dripping through and soaking their clothes.

Clara slept, then woke up sobbing, "Mummy, please come and take me home. Mummy. I'm cold. I'm hungry."

"Shush. Go to sleep, Clara," Charlie muttered.

"I can't sleep. I'm soaked and freezing. It's almost morning, so let's just get up. Nothing is worse than trying to sleep in a pool of water."

Clara crawled out into the drizzle and darkness of the forest.

"Which way do we go, Charlie? I can't see the mountains anymore."

"I marked the tree ahead. See that bit of cloth. That's the way. That's east and should take us to the trail."

Clara and Charlie looked like they had escaped from a war zone. Their hair was matted from the rain; their clothes were torn and soaked; there were numerous scratches on their arms and legs; and Charlie's face was blotchy with bites. Worse were the sharp thorns from devil's club, the forest plant that grew taller than the children and scratched their arms and faces, leaving tiny barbs in their flesh if they grabbed the branches.

The next few hours were tortuous as they struggled through the wet forest.

"We've been walking for hours, Charlie. I need to rest, and I need food," Clara said, now moving at a snail's pace.

"We gotta go a bit further before we eat. There's not much left. I'm so hungry I could eat leaves if I thought they wouldn't kill me," Charlie said, as he staggered forward.

"There are forest plants I love to eat. My mom teaches me lots about plants when we go out gathering roots, mushrooms and berries. The best are the bear roots. In the spring, they taste just like carrots. This time of year, we might be able to find berries. Mom and I pick blueberries and cranberries not far from our house."

"Please find a berry patch. This is the first time in my life I haven't eaten at least six times in a day," Charlie said. "Now all we have to split is a quarter of a sandwich, an eighth each, right? Imagine learning math out here in the middle of nowhere," Charlie laughed.

"How are we going to find our way? I read that people who are lost and can't see the sun or any landmarks just keep going around in circles."

"We should find a creek. Water flows into water, and little creeks become bigger creeks, and eventually, they flow into the Yukon River. The trail goes along the river, so a creek should lead us to the Telegraph Trail. 'Elementary, dear Watson,' detective Sherlock said."

"You must like reading Sherlock Holmes. You're always talking about him. I like to read Charles Dickens, and right now I'm reading *Anne of Green Gables*."

"Yuk! My sister read that to me. It was so sickening, I just about threw up. She is such a goody-goody…'lessons to be learned and honors to be won.'"

"Who are you talking about? Anne of Green Gables or your sister?"

"Both. When Victoria read that line, 'lessons to be learned and honors to be won,'" Charlie chanted the phrase in a mocking voice, "that was when I told my big sis that I would read to myself. Since then Sherlock Holmes, the great detective, and the space traveller Buck Rogers have kept me safe from those silly girly books."

"I love those books and would like to be just like Anne and your sister. I want to do something with my life, maybe become a teacher like Anne and live in Whitehorse in a house with running water, a garden and a fence."

"Wow, a teacher! Now, that's ambition. I hate teachers."

"You have a bit of a chip on your shoulder, as my dad would say, and sometimes you're not so easy to be with. If we are out here in the middle of the forest, I think you should try and understand what another person might like. I don't tell you that stories about Buck Rogers are stupid and that you don't learn anything from reading about space travel, which everyone knows will never happen."

"You're telling me right now that you don't like me or what I like, and you adore my prissy sister. People will go into space. They will invent all sorts of neat things like being able to send pictures to a machine in your home, so you can watch movies in your living room and watch the news instead of just listening to the radio."

"You should spend more time studying in school and less time reading detective stories and space fantasies, or you'll get nowhere in life. My mom says that getting a good education is the most important thing."

"Sometimes, Clara, you use your book learning too much and don't use your head enough. That's what will get you into trouble."

"And what about you? The sun sets in the east? Now where would you be if I wasn't here with my book learning?"

"I give up. Girls! You're all the same. Just a gaggle of know-it-alls." He picked up his pace and crashed through the bush, not bothering to wait for Clara.

Hot tears rolled down Clara's face. She mulled angry words over in her mind. *What a useless, unbearable, stupid boy! How could he talk to me like that? I'll put him in his place. I'll tell Edward what he said, and Edward will flatten his stupid, ugly, bug-bitten face.*

Clara dropped behind as the angry thoughts burned up the limited energy she had left in her frail body. *I just hate him. I hate him.* Now she was really crying. Sobs erupted, and tears poured down her face. She stopped to sit down, exhausted by the outpouring of anger.

When Clara stood up, Charlie was not in sight. *He's just ahead,* she thought, as she stumbled through the thick bush. Her eyes were glued to the forest ahead, hoping to catch a glimpse of Charlie's blue backpack.

Now he's done it! He left me behind, and now we're not only lost, we're separated!

Clara was still angry at Charlie, not just for the argument, but for leaving her. She had never been alone in the forest before. The rain had stopped, and the wind picked up and sped through the tall spruce trees.

Her anger and frustration overwhelmed her. She could not think clearly, and she plunged through the woods without watching where she was stepping. Sharp branches scraped across her body. One narrowly missed an eye, leaving a cut on her cheek. Blood trickled from the wound, mixing with her tears. Rather than slowing down, she picked up her pace, running through the dark forest and jumping over the deadfall. Pieces of her clothing tore off in her mad rush, and her slight body poured with perspiration.

"Charlie! Charlie! Wait for me! Don't leave me alone!" She crashed through the woods, creating so much noise that her weak cries were drowned out.

In any case, Charlie was now too far away to hear her. He turned to check on Clara and was about to say something to make her laugh, to make her not hate him, when he realized she wasn't behind him.

"Clara! Clara! Where are you? I'm sorry! I didn't mean what I said. Clara! Please!"

The forest closed in around him. Trees and bush everywhere. Now he didn't know where he had been going or where Clara might be. Charlie stood for a long time, calling Clara and hoping she would hear him.

It wasn't so bad when they were together. At least they had each other, and he always felt that they would eventually find the Telegraph Trail or the Yukon River. Now the dreadful possibility of being lost forever or dying out here in the forest came over him. He missed Victoria.

If only we'd had kept the Telegraph Trail in sight! If only I had stayed with Clara. Together we could survive, he thought grimly.

Clara felt even more terrified than Charlie as she continued her headlong rush through the bush. Fear and anger gave her the energy to keep running, and she stumbled through the dense underbrush not caring how many branches scratched her or how many mosquitoes sucked blood from her neck. She was beyond pain; she was filled with dread and anger.

In her panic, she didn't notice the change in terrain and suddenly found herself at the top of a hill. She didn't pause but continued her mad rush over the hilltop. Suddenly, she was running downhill through the pine trees. Then the tree cover disappeared, and she was in the open on a steep slope. She didn't think to slow down and move carefully across the slippery shale on the valley side. Her feet came out from under her, and down she went, sliding across the sharp scree of rocks, trying to catch a foothold with her soggy sneakers. Her backpack dug into her, and rocks scraped her body. She tried to grab a willow to stop her downward slide, but the shallow roots pulled out. She slid until her elbow smashed against a log at the bottom of the hill.

"Ouch! Ouch! You rotten log! You crummy, good-for-nothing log! I don't want to be here! I want to go home. Charlie! Where are you? Darn it, anyway!" A storm of tears poured down her cheeks. She sat rocking back and forth, her arm throbbing with pain. Then she saw the blood. There was a deep gash above her elbow. "My arm's hurt! My arm's hurt!" she sobbed.

Clara sat weeping in agony, and for a time, was unable to move. Finally, she crawled under the sheltering branches of a fir tree, hoping that if she lay down, the throbbing pain would stop. She sobbed quietly, not even thinking of what she would do next. She had given up. She would let the forest take her. Eventually, she fell into an exhausted sleep, enveloped by the dark forest.

Realizing he was separated from Clara, Charlie circled back, trying to retrace his path. He walked slowly, stopping every few minutes to call for Clara. He had a sick feeling in his stomach.

If only I hadn't argued with Clara. Why did I have to call her names? He plodded along, scolding himself and regretting every mean word he had said.

But it was impossible for Charlie to retrace his steps. He couldn't remember whether he'd gone east, west, south or north. He kept calling Clara's name, trying to make his voice heard above the howling wind, his voice growing hoarse with the effort.

Charlie became more and more dejected. He blamed himself for arguing with Clara, and as he continued walking, hour after hour, he realized he had no idea whether he should go straight, turn left, go back or turn right. He was truly lost. He paused again to call out. He looked through the dark and gloomy woods. All the trees and bushes looked the same. A branch snapped in the distance.

"Clara! Is that you?" he yelled.

"Clara!" He heard only the rustle of the trees and then, again, the sound of something moving through the forest. "Clara!" Charlie yelled again.

He would be so relieved if only it was his friend Clara, and together they could find their way out of the forest. But relief turned to terror when a grizzly bear emerged through the trees. The bear moved closer, and Charlie could see the foam dripping from its jaws. The grizzly reared up on its hind legs, towering above the small boy. It was so enormous its head would have touched the ceiling of Charlie's bedroom back in Whitehorse. It rolled its head from side to side, huffing at Charlie and sniffing the air.

Charlie stopped breathing. Then he whispered, "Drop and roll," the only emergency response that Charlie could remember. He fell to the ground and rolled away from the grizzly, curling up into a tight ball. He could hear the bear approach but was too terrified to look. He wrapped his arms about his head and tucked his knees into his stomach. He waited motionless, his heart pounding.

He heard the bear move. Closer and closer it came. Its heavy footsteps reverberated through the ground. Charlie knew it would come for him, paw him and then chew. Now he could smell the grizzly's heavy, hot breath. He would not die quickly. It would eat his arm or leg while he screamed in pain. He would be eaten while he was still alive.

Please just kill me quickly.

Charlie remained curled up in a ball, paralyzed with fear. The bear sniffed and then nudged Charlie with its nose, rolling the boy over on the ground.

This is the end. If only I had stayed with Clara. If only..., Charlie choked back a sob and prayed. *Please move time back a week, and I will change.* But time stayed still, and Charlie waited for the end.

Uncle Joe had been tracking the children all day with no luck. Darkness swept into the thick forest.

"We will need something to eat," Uncle Joe said. "I want the two of you to start a fire and make coffee. A drink of that caffeine, and I can go all night. I'll build you a shelter." The trapper quickly erected poles, threw a tarp over the structure, creating a cozy dry bush tent.

Victoria was more than relieved to get out of the rain and rest for a while. Cold, hunger, worry and exertion were taking their toll. She sank down on the forest floor where Uncle Joe had placed a ground sheet and a blanket. "We'll heat up the can of beans and have fresh coffee ready for you!" she called out. But Uncle Joe and Bruiser had already disappeared into the dense, dark forest.

Edward returned with firewood, to find Victoria still resting. "Sorry. I don't mean to be lazy," she explained. "I am just so tired, I can barely move".

"Here, take my coat and keep warm. You'll need some sleep if we're to continue the search."

"I should help you keep the fire going," Victoria protested.

"I think Uncle will be gone some time, and I'll be bored waiting. I would rather have something to do, so please rest."

Victoria welcomed the chance to lie down and soon fell asleep.

Chapter IX

Grizzly Tale

Victoria slept fitfully, disturbed by frightening nightmares. She woke with a jolt when Uncle Joe returned.

"I have to tell you something that will upset you," he said. "Not far from here, I discovered that the two children are no longer travelling together. There is one set of footprints heading north. That's Clara. There's another set heading off to the east. That is your brother," Joe said to Victoria. "He will get to the Telegraph Trail if he keeps on his current direction. It's Clara I am worried about."

"I think it best if you two stay here while I try to find Clara. The footprints are fresh. They must have split up earlier today. I don't know why. Maybe Clara dropped behind. Maybe they had an argument. We will find them both once there is more light. Will you both stay in the camp until I get back?"

"I want to come with you, Uncle Joe. Maybe I could find Charlie's footprints. I've been learning how to track." Edward could not bear the thought of the two lost and alone in the woods for another night.

"It would be better if you and Victoria rested. It would also help if you could keep the fire burning because if I find the children, they will need a fire for warmth and some hot food. Stay. It is best." Uncle Joe gulped half of his coffee before moving quietly into the bush again, not waiting for a reply.

"I can't sleep anymore. Why don't you have a rest, and I'll keep the fire going," Victoria suggested.

Victoria sat in the bush tent, watching the glowing embers of the fire. Edward slept while Victoria occasionally rose to gather more wood. She worried about Charlie and Clara, and prayed for their safety.

Charlie was far from safe. He was terrified and dizzy with fear, certain that the bear intended to eat him. He remembered a story he'd heard about a miner. A hungry grizzly pulled him out of a tree, chewed the miner's leg off and buried the poor man under a pile of dirt. After a few days, the man died, and his body was a tender meal for the bear. Charlie remembered hearing that grizzlies buried their prey before they ate them. And that would be his fate. He would never see his sister or father again. He would be eaten. Clara would die alone in the woods, and it was all his fault. He choked back a sob and closed his eyes to await his fate.

The grizzly nudged the small, curled-up boy, huffing and sniffing. Charlie's heart pounded. Once more the bear rose up on its hind legs as if preparing to come in for the kill. Then

Charlie heard heavy footsteps reverberating through the ground. He closed his eyes; his heart almost stopped. Seconds passed, then a minute. Charlie couldn't look. If he opened his eyes, would he see the grizzly closing in on him, its huge teeth and foaming mouth ready for the kill?

I have to look. Charlie forced open his eyes. Blood pounded in his veins. *Is this the end?*

But the great beast was no longer stalking the boy about to enjoy a tasty supper. What Charlie saw was the butt of the grizzly as it shuffled away into the forest. Relief flooded through Charlie's body.

He's leaving! He's not going to eat me! I'm alive! Charlie was filled with relief and the simple joy of being alive, of having escaped death. He did not feel hungry and, for the moment, he even forgot his concerns for Clara. Once he was sure the bear was far enough away, he slowly got up off the ground. Then he giggled to himself.

"Drop and roll," he said, his voice squeakily. He laughed and then repeated, "Drop and roll." He giggled again. "I may have had my emergency responses mixed up, but what the heck. It worked!"

It was too dark to continue on through the forest. Charlie decided to crawl under a fir tree and sleep until first light. He knew he would find his way out somehow. When he did, he would get a search party to find Clara, and that would make up for every bad word he'd said and all the terrible things he'd done.

Escaping death by grizzly had given Charlie renewed energy and hope. When he woke the next day, he looked around and thought about his predicament. He no longer felt he would have any chance of finding Clara on his own. He had to go for help. He had to find the Telegraph Trail. He sat on a log and looked around. The sky had cleared, and the first faint rays of the morning sun lit up the eastern horizon in shades of red.

"Okay, the sun rises in the east, and the Yukon River is east. That is where the trail is. I need a landmark," Charlie said, speaking softly and calmly to himself.

Charlie found a tall, old fir tree and scrambled up the trunk, getting footholds on the big branches. The boughs scratched his arms and face, but he paid little attention to the pain, concentrating on getting a firm foothold. Despite the dim morning light, he could make out a series of cliffs to the east. As the morning sun touched the cliff tops, he chose a scraggy peak in the east.

"I will call you my Craggy Cliffs, and I will follow you till you lead me to the river," he announced. The shape of the cliffs was etched in his mind.

Clara, exhausted and starving, no longer had the energy to crawl out from her hiding place under the fir tree. Although her arm hurt, if she didn't move, the pain was bearable. She slept, woke briefly and fell back asleep again. The cold seeped into her thin, starving body. She no longer had the will to live. When she woke for a few minutes, Clara thought of her warm home and about her kind mother. She sobbed and fell back into a fitful sleep.

She woke to the noise of something crashing through the bush. The branches parted, and something brushed against her foot. She screamed. But it wasn't a bear. It was only a couple of red squirrels rustling the branches as they jumped from branch to branch.

Fear drained the last of Clara's energy. She felt faint and couldn't move. She believed that this hiding place would be her grave. Summer would pass, and then the bitter cold of winter would set in. Hungry wolves would eat her, and next summer, all that would remain would be her bones.

Clara was no longer aware of anything around her. She drifted in and out of consciousness. She did not hear footsteps. And if she had heard her uncle moving through the woods, she no longer had the energy to make herself heard.

It was dark, and Uncle Joe was having trouble tracing his niece's footsteps. "Poor child," he muttered when he noticed blood near her footprints. "She must be injured and can barely walk. Now, where has she gone?"

He ran his fingers over the ground, trying to find the next footprint. Bruiser was running through the bush chasing the same red squirrels that had frightened Clara. Joe crouched for a few minutes, trying to figure out why Clara's footprints had disappeared. He got to his feet and returned to the last print he had seen beside the big tree.

It's just too dark, he thought, and he turned back towards the bush camp to rejoin Edward and Victoria and wait until the morning light to resume his search.

Clara heard his footsteps. She tried to call out but couldn't make a sound. It was as if someone had a vice-like grip on her throat. Then she cried out, with a sound like the mewl of a tiny kitten, but her voice was muffled by the sound of Bruiser running through the bushes.

"Come, Bruiser," he yelled. Uncle Joe moved away from where Clara lay dying beneath the tree branches. Bruiser bounded through the woods, passing near the tree.

"Bruiser! Let's go," Joe yelled. Then he noticed the big dog sniffing around the tree. Joe was about to call the dog again when Bruiser disappeared under the branches. "What have you found there?"

Joe heard a faint whimper. He ran to the tree, pulled aside the branches and saw his little niece curled up in a ball on the ground.

The first signs of morning had lit the sky when Victoria saw Uncle Joe approach the camp, carrying Clara in his arms.

Edward woke with a jolt.

"You found them!" Edward yelled, tears of relief filling his eyes.

"I found Clara," Joe said, gently laying the unconscious girl on Edward's jacket.

"Was there any sign of Charlie?" Victoria was frantic.

"Now don't fret too much about your brother. He was headed in the right direction and may reach the trail before I find him," Uncle Joe said. "Clara needs your help now. Once she is out of danger, you can ask her about Charlie. But she needs care. She's starving and cold, and she has a bad cut on her arm."

Joe's words were enough to get Victoria to focus on Clara.

"You poor dear," Victoria said soothingly. "I'll just clean up those cuts and put soft bandages over them. Soon we'll have you better." Although Victoria spoke calmly, she shivered when she saw the deep gash on Clara's arm.

Clara didn't speak as Victoria patched her wounds. Edward stirred up the embers of the campfire to make tea and soup. They were able to rouse Clara long enough for her to sip a little sweetened tea before she fell back to sleep. Edward sat near his little sister, holding her hand to reassure her should she dream that she was still alone in the woods.

"Here's the plan," Uncle Joe said in a quiet voice as they sat around the fire. "Once we have our breakfast, I'll take you out to the Telegraph Trail. From there, the two of you can carry Clara to my cabin and look after her. If she doesn't recover soon, take her to the fort in my boat. I'll double back and keep searching for Charlie. Bruiser and I'll go back to where the two of them split up."

They broke camp, put out the fire and, with Clara in her uncle's strong arms, they headed to the Telegraph Trail. They did not have to track now, and within an hour after leaving the bush camp, they were on the trail. Uncle Joe lifted Clara into Edward's arms and disappeared back into the woods.

"Wait!" Victoria called. "What if *you* get lost?"

But he was already gone, and it was a question that didn't need an answer. In these woods, Uncle Joe would never get lost. In these woods, there were few animals, let alone humans, that Uncle Joe could not track.

Chapter X

The Craggy Cliffs

Charlie's emotions swung from sheer joy at escaping the bear to overwhelming guilt over his mean words to Clara, words that had caused them to split up, words that had left his friend alone in the forest. Now his concern for Clara drove him. But he no longer dashed through the woods. He had a plan. He stopped often to make sure his landmark was still in sight. If he couldn't see the cliffs, he would climb a tree to get a clear view.

"Craggy Cliffs," he would say, "you are still there showing me the way. Clara, hold on. We'll find you. Stay safe. Don't give up."

As Charlie made his way east, he crossed a small creek. *Little creeks flow into bigger creeks and then into rivers.* He paused, looking up at his faithful cliffs that poked above the trees. He stood for some time beside the small stream, taking several gulps and splashing his itchy bites.

Beaver fever! No way! This water is as pure as rain from heaven! The water did little to fill his empty stomach.

"I think I should follow the stream, but I'll keep my Craggy Cliffs in sight just in case."

The stream bounced across rocks, weaving between willows. On higher ground, the forest was carpeted with lichen, that frothy-looking plant that the caribou eat. Suddenly there, nestled among the lichen, were bushes loaded with blueberries.

"Thank you, little stream!" Charlie grabbed handfuls of the ripe berries, stuffing them in his mouth. "Yum! Yum! So good for my tum!" he hummed as he grazed on the berries. After two days with little food, the berries tasted sweeter than anything he had ever eaten in his life. Once he'd had his fill of berries and water, Charlie lay in the sun enjoying the feeling of a full stomach. He started to drift off to sleep, when guilt and worry washed over him.

"Clara, I'm sorry. I'll only take little catnaps from now on." Charlie bounced to his feet and rummaged through his pack. "Okay, where is my water bottle?"

He emptied his backpack piece by piece—sandwich wrappers, his windbreaker, the first aid kit, a pocketknife and the empty water bottle. The last item was a brown leather sack that was so heavy it plopped down with a thump on the ground. He opened the drawstring and lifted out a large gold nugget.

He put the nugget against his lips. "If only I could use this gold to find Clara. Maybe when I get to Fort Selkirk, it will help to have the gold. Otherwise, I would leave you behind, but then someday, I would hate myself for giving you up and going through all of this for nothing. I just want to get out of the forest, find Clara and then I'll use the money to get her the biggest present she has ever had."

He daydreamed of buying a fluffy, stuffed dog for Clara or maybe he'd even be brave and buy her a pretty dress. He put the nugget into the bag and replaced it in his backpack.

With those pleasant visions in his head, he filled the bottle with berries, packing them tightly into the container. "You never know when I'll get my next meal." After a few more mouthfuls of berries, Charlie headed along the creek. At first the going was easy. He walked along the hillside on a narrow animal trail.

Occasionally, other creeks bubbled down to join the main stream. The trail veered off, heading away from the Craggy Cliffs. Charlie looked back uneasily, realizing that he was breaking his promise to continue straight east and keep the Craggy Cliffs in sight. Each time he glanced back, the cliffs were farther away. The next time he looked, they were out of sight.

Ahead, the valley widened, and the creek meandered, weaving back and forth. The ground was wet, and moss grew along the creek banks. Another tiny stream flowed down into the valley through a tangle of trees and bush. Charlie had to wrestle his way through the willows to cross the little stream. He continued for an hour through the valley, keeping a short distance from the creek.

As he struggled on, he repeated to himself, "Small creeks have to run into big creeks and then eventually to the Yukon River. This is my lucky creek."

But already Charlie began to wonder if the creek was indeed lucky or instead, deviously offering him food, then leading him farther and farther from safety. He continued to follow the creek as it widened and flowed into a broad valley. A narrow game trail wound through thorny devil's club, leading him to a thick barrier of bush. Charlie pushed his way through a tangle of willows and emerged on the edge of a marshy expanse.

He had hoped that the little stream he was following would become a big stream and that the land would drop down towards the Yukon River. This was not what he saw. Before him was a wide valley covered in swamp and marsh. Shallow water stretched before him into the distance, and the creek he had been following disappeared into the wetlands.

Charlie could not accept that he had made such a disastrous mistake, that the cheerful little forest stream could have led him into this mess. He stood at the edge of the swamp and pondered his predicament.

"Do I go through the swamp and hope a stream runs out of the marsh and into the Yukon River, or do I turn back and find the path to the Craggy Cliffs? Yikes! I'm being eaten alive, so I have to do something before these mosquitoes drain all my blood."

He stepped into the cold, sluggish water. His foot sank into the oozy bottom, and he jumped back onto the mossy bank.

"No way! I am not plowing through this muck so the bugs can have their fill." Charlie slapped at a dozen mosquitoes that sucked on his neck and face. "No bugs and marsh for me!"

Disheartened, Charlie turned back and pushed his way through the thick cluster of willows. His hand closed around a branch of devil's club, impaling it with a bunch of thorns. He was at a low point, having wasted precious time. He needed to reach help for Clara. It took over an hour for Charlie to retrace his steps.

"I will no longer get distracted. The Craggy Cliffs will show me the way."

Charlie looked eastward to catch a glimpse of the cliffs, but the tall trees masked his view. Even after climbing a large tree, he was unable to see anything but more tree tops.

"Where did I last see you? At the first stream crossing? Yes, I think that was it."

Charlie was tired from the fruitless hike along the stream, but he plodded along, looking up every few minutes in search of the Craggy Cliffs. When he reached the first stream crossing, he was sure he would see the cliffs. But clouds had moved across the sky, sank into the valley and blocked the view.

"Time for a rest," Charlie announced. "If I don't see the cliffs when I wake up, I could be lost forever and never find Clara and never get home again." Never getting home again meant dying out here alone and lost in the forest, and he did not want to put those dreadful thoughts into words.

He pulled out his windbreaker, found a sheltered spot under a tree and curled up for a nap. When he woke, the forest was washed in moonlight, and the trees gave off eerie shadows. He gathered up his belongings, took a drink from the little stream and looked about, spotting a massive fir tree just ahead.

Charlie scrambled up the big fir. "Too many branches!"

Charlie moved carefully to the other side of the tree and pushed aside the boughs. There they were, the Craggy Cliffs, starkly outlined in the moonlight. Charlie felt reassured. Once again, he had his landmark in sight.

Edward carried Clara to Uncle Joe's cabin and placed her gently on a cot. Victoria fussed over her young friend while Edward looked after the fire and heated up some soup.

Clara slept fitfully that night, while her brother and Victoria took turns caring for her. When Edward was on watch, Clara tossed in her bunk and whimpered.

"It's okay, little sis. You're safe now. Sleep and get better."

But she did not get better. The tiny girl thrashed about, sometimes shivering from cold and then pushing her blankets aside as her fever spiked. When it was Victoria's turn to watch over the sick girl, she gently placed her fingers on Clara's forehead.

"Edward! Wake up! I think Clara is really sick, and I can't do anything more to help her. She is burning up with fever."

"Wow! She's burning hot. Did you look in Uncle Joe's cupboards for medicine? Aspirin might work."

"I don't think your uncle ever gets sick. There's no medicine in the cupboards. He doesn't even use store-bought toothpaste. It looks like he uses baking soda to brush his teeth and cure all ills. I'll try and lower her temperature with a cool cloth, but if that doesn't work, we'll have to take her to Fort Selkirk. Is there a doctor there?"

"No doctor, but my auntie lives there and knows all the old cures. There is also Mrs. Fogbottle, a bossy, unpleasant woman who runs the clinic and has a cupboard full of medicine."

"That gash on her arm looks infected and will only get worse. Edward, could you get the boat ready while I pack supplies? We'll probably be away for a few days, so leave a note for your uncle."

"Did you know that you are starting to boss me around just like I was your little brother, and I don't even mind that much," he said, as he scribbled the note. "I'll get the boat ready. It has a powerful motor, so we'll be at the fort in no time."

Despite the strain of the night, Victoria smiled at her companion. "If we make it through this with everyone safe, I'll hike to Dawson City with you, and I will never bristle when you suggest I eat more food or wear better boots. I even believe Charlie will make it to safety. What do you think?"

"I'm sure Uncle Joe will find your brother and bring him home. Once, he tracked a moose for ten days, living off the food he collected in the woods. He'll find Charlie, and because your brother has more energy than ten people, he'll survive."

They loaded the supplies and made a comfortable bed for Clara in the bottom of the boat. The night was lit by a bright moon as Edward carried his sister down the riverbank. The motor roared as the boat headed to civilization, medicine and help.

Charlie felt energized now that he had rested, and his landmark was in sight. When he saw the cliffs from the tree perch, he took his bearings from the position of the moon and stars and pushed off through the bush.

"Big Dipper straight ahead and three stars like a belt, directly behind."

When he could not see the Craggy Cliffs from the ground, he climbed a tree to get his bearings, and carried on, his path lit by moonlight. The night was cool, but Charlie kept warm by moving quickly through the forest. Every hour or two, he would climb a tree or find an open area to confirm his direction.

"I can see you, Craggy Cliffs! You are so close now!" he exclaimed, from his viewpoint high on the tree. Then, near the cliffs, he saw a sight that filled him with sheer joy. In the distance was the moonlit silver ribbon of water. It was the Yukon River. "I'm going to be saved, and I'm going to help them find Clara!"

Hopefully there are boats on the river and people who can help. Maybe there's a cabin, and someone will give me a moose meat sandwich and maybe apple pie! Charlie had to restrain himself to keep from dashing through the bush towards the river.

As he continued through the night, the moon sank below the horizon. The forest was dark, and the night grew colder. Charlie moved cautiously through the heavy underbrush, taking care not to stumble. He glanced up at the stars.

Big dipper and those three stars. What are they called in that Buck Rogers book? Orion's belt. Yes! I can learn from books, just like Clara.

He did not stop to sleep, but as the night wore on, his pace slowed. Finally, a dim light appeared in the east, announcing the new day.

I'll reach the Telegraph Trail, Craggy Cliffs, and then the Yukon River. I will find people to search for Clara. It can't be far now. Hold on, Clara. Hold on!

He stumbled through the woods until the sunlight broke over the mountains.

If only I could get out to the river and find help for Clara.

As he struggled along, tired and hungry, he imagined he could hear voices. Charlie paused and listened but heard only the sound of the birds and the rustling of the branches in the wind. Then he stumbled into an opening.

It's the Telegraph Trail! But once again he was disappointed. It was a just game trail and a small clearing created where the moose had grazed and rested.

The Telegraph Trail had to be near the river. Wasn't it between me and the river? It had to be, but why is it taking so long to find it?

He plodded on, trying to keep up the pace without going so fast that he risked an injury. His legs felt like jelly. During the night, he had sucked the last drops of berry juice from his water jar. Now his mouth was dry, his lips parched, and his throat seemed to be on fire.

I am just so thirsty and hungry. I will be fine once I get to the river, drink ten cups of water and find people with a boat, people who have lots of food.

Charlie was becoming weaker. It became increasingly difficult for him to climb over the fallen logs and crawl through the thick underbrush. As he trudged on, Charlie caught his foot on a root, and he crashed to the ground.

"Ouch! Stupid tree with your stupid roots! I've just about had enough!" He was close to tears as he tried to gain enough strength to get to his feet and push on.

"I promise not to give up, Clara. I won't sleep until I find some help."

His determination kept him moving, although he had no energy. He was feeling ill, and his head felt like it was on fire. All he could do was put one foot ahead of the other. He struggled through a grove of willows and thick underbrush, but he could find no tall fir trees to climb. As the hours passed, he wondered if he had indeed seen the river or if it had been a figment of his imagination, a sight his brain conjured up to make him rush off in the wrong direction.

I'm never going to find the trail or the river, and I'll never see my sister again, and if Clara dies in the forest, it will be my fault!

Chapter XI

Fort Selkirk

As Charlie tortured himself with feelings of guilt for placing Clara in such danger, the girl who was in his thoughts was very ill. Edward pushed the motor to its highest speed, anxious to reach help for his sister. Victoria watched over the sick girl, moistening her brow with a cool cloth to contain the fever.

"We're not far from the fort," Edward said. "It won't be long before we can get help for Clara."

When they finally reached Fort Selkirk, they pulled up alongside several boats moored at the docks. Edward jumped onto the dock, tied up the boat, then reached out to take Clara from Victoria, who gently lifted the sick girl into Edward's arms. She then picked up their few belongings and followed as Edward took long strides up the steep bank to the fort.

"We'll take her to Auntie's. She'll be more comfortable there."

Early morning light beamed over the high cliffs on the far side of the river, illuminating the row of neat buildings that made up Fort Selkirk. They crossed a wide expanse of grass and walked past the Hudson's Bay Store, a church, the Savoie Hotel and the Royal Canadian Mounted Police headquarters. At the far end of the village centre was a group of small, sturdy log houses.

"Auntie!" he called, as he knocked on the door of a small, neat cabin. "Sorry to wake you, but we need your help."

A middle-aged, plump Tutchone woman opened the door, still bleary-eyed from sleep. "Edward. What have you brought me? This isn't my niece, is it?" she asked in a worried voice. "Bring her in, and let me see what's wrong."

"It's her arm, Ma'am," Victoria said.

"And who would this so-called medicine woman be?"

"Auntie, this is Victoria, Captain Russell's daughter. She has been helping me look after Clara since Uncle Joe found her in the woods. She's taken very good care of Clara, but she doesn't know the medicines like you do. Victoria, this is my Auntie Violet."

"Hmmph," was Aunt Violet's only greeting. "Bring Clara over to the bed near the window so I can see if it is her arm as the young miss believes."

"I didn't mean to pretend I know anything about healing, I...," Victoria didn't know what to say to this self-assured Indigenous woman, who was obviously holding some grudge against teenage girls, or possibly against anyone with fair skin.

"Oh my! Oh, poor little dear," Aunt Violet moaned, as she examined her niece. "Edward, put the kettle on the stove, and you," she motioned to Victoria, "fetch me the comfrey from that green bowl." She pointed in the general direction of the kitchen shelf where a row of bowls, baskets and bottles lined the wall, all neatly labeled.

Victoria searched the shelf, nervous and somewhat taken aback by Violet's attitude towards her. "Is this what you want?"

"That's baking powder. Are you all there, girl? No. To your right, where the herbs are. I need the comfrey. Now, find a small bowl where I can mix up the medicine for this child. Look in the cupboard above your head." While Aunt Violet ordered them around, she continued to check Clara over, clucking over her niece's injuries like a worried mother hen. She was gentle and caring with Clara, and sharp-tongued when speaking to Victoria.

"I will make a poultice with the comfrey and brew spruce tea to bring down her fever. Edward, could you bring in more wood? I will have to boil water, and you," she once again nailed Victoria with her eyes, "find the basket with the spruce needles and put a few pinches into the teapot."

This time Victoria found the small, beautifully woven basket and carried out Violet's orders quickly, although with some apprehension that the slightest mistake would cause renewed scowls.

"Is it all right if I help Edward with the wood? I am finding it a little hot in here."

"Go, Miss. I can look after Clara."

Victoria ran over to where Edward was chopping wood. "What has your aunt got against me? She hates me. I thought you said it was Mrs. Fogbottle who was difficult to deal with? Your aunt is not even giving me a chance."

"She has her reasons—something to do with a difference over the care of a little baby. She still thinks anyone outside of our group has no respect for her healing skills because one day a Tutchone baby was taken to Whitehorse, where the little girl died. Her mother never saw the baby again, not even to bury the poor child." He paused as he thought about the anguish the parents felt. "She figured you come from Whitehorse, and so you're partly to blame."

"That's terrible. I guess I can understand why she doesn't trust me."

"She is a great healer, and when she needs modern medicine, she is not too proud to go to Mrs. Fogbottle for help, although I wouldn't want to be around when those two meet. It is like two lightning bolts clashing."

"I will try to hold my tongue and help your aunt look after Clara. All I want is for your sister to get well, and to know that Charlie is safe with Joe."

They returned to the overheated cabin and watched Aunt Violet mix the poultice for Clara's arm. She was very gentle with Clara, speaking softly to the sick girl in the Tutchone language as she applied the mixture of herbs to the deep gash on Clara's arm.

"Have you made the tea? Good. Bring me half a cup, and I will try and get Clara to drink a few sips. Make sure it is not too hot. I don't want you burning her throat. It should be hot, but not too hot."

Victoria tried to figure out what "hot but not too hot" meant. She dipped her finger in the tea to test it.

"Don't do that," Violet scolded. "You want this child to get more germs? Throw that out and pour fresh tea. To test the temperature, sprinkle a little tea on your wrist using a teaspoon. I would think you would know that."

"I'm sorry. You're right. I haven't had a mother to help me, and I don't mind if you tell me how you want things done."

This seemed to soften Aunt Violet. "I know, child, and I shouldn't be so hard on you. You've done your best for Clara, and we will have her better in no time. Let's try this tea, and if her fever doesn't go down, maybe I could get you to make the trip over to the missus who has all the expensive medicine that she reluctantly shares with us folks."

"Do you mean Mrs. Fogbottle?"

"There is no one else around here that has a cupboard full of medicine large enough to cure the Canadian army, should it ever pass through Fort Selkirk. She will bite your head off as soon as speak to you, but I would rather have you deal with her than send Edward. As everyone knows, my nephew may look like his Scottish father, but she knows he is Tutchone. That battle-axe would have sent Edward and Clara two hundred miles away to residential school if I hadn't put her in her place and proved that their parents had every bit as much education as any of the teachers in Whitehorse. If I went over there, I would tell the old biddy what I think of her and her ways of snatching our children and sending them God knows where to die."

"Now, Auntie, try not to get worked up. How is Clara's temperature?"

"Still feverish, I'm afraid. Let's give her time to rest. She drank a few sips of the tea, and it will take time to work. You children must be hungry. Let's have a cup of real tea and some of that bannock, then maybe Clara will come around."

But the fever did not drop, and Auntie Violet sent Victoria across to the building where Mrs. Fogbottle ruled over a clinic, dispensing advice and medicine.

She knocked on the door and stood nervously on the steps, expecting the worse. Instead of Mrs. Fogbottle, a tall policeman smiled down at her.

"Oh! Is Mrs. Fogbottle here? We have a sick child over at Auntie Violet's, and we need antibiotics."

"I can't help you. I just dropped in to see if there were any patients under Mrs. Fogbottle's care. Corporal Greer's the name, and who would you be?"

"Victoria Russell, Sir."

"Aye, then you must be Captain Russell's daughter. Well, Mrs. Fogbottle must be at church, but she should be back shortly. She will have to look after this. I heard some story about children lost in the woods. I guess Joe Jack found the girl. Is that the sick one? I hear they haven't found the boy yet. Would that be your brother?" He spoke in a rapid-fire voice that was not unpleasant, but monotone and businesslike.

"Yes, but how do you know he is still lost? I was certain Uncle Joe would find him, and that Charlie would be safe. Edward's Uncle Joe is so good at tracking." Victoria's voice cracked with emotion.

"Well, I don't know the whole story. I am supposed to be informed when children go missing. Instead, it seems I am the last to know. Anyway, a boat came from Uncle Joe's cabin with word that the boy is still missing. That is all I know for now, but next time, please come to see me when someone is lost? It is my job to get a search party underway, not Joe's."

"Yes, Sir. I am sorry, but we thought..."

"Don't try and take the law into your hands. You are just youngsters and should leave matters up to the Royal Canadian Mounted Police. That's our job. And leave the nursing up to Mrs. Fogbottle; that's her domain. Not that Auntie Violet isn't one of the best when it comes to figuring what is wrong with a person, but sick people need to be in the clinic and need modern medicine, not herbs and such. Speaking of the missus, I think I hear her now."

The door opened, and a tall, imposing woman entered, hymn book in her hand and a puzzled look on her severe face.

"Gertrude, this is Victoria. Violet sent her for some medicine."

"And who is it that needs this medicine, and why isn't the patient here under my care?"

"It's Violet's niece, Clara," Victoria answered. "She was lost in the forest for two days and has an infected cut on her arm. Violet would like some antibiotics if you could spare a little."

"Oh, she would, would she?" She placed her arms on her ample hips. "I would think she would come herself with this kind of request. Instead, she seems to believe the child is in better hands with ancient medicines, but when that doesn't work she is after my cures. Tell her the child has to be brought to the clinic, and then we shall see if she needs antibiotics. I am not in the habit of giving out medicine to anyone knocking on my door."

"Clara is very sick, Ma'am, and I don't think she should be moved. My father will be back soon when the ship returns from Dawson City, and I guess we'll just have to wait until he comes. The medical officer on the ship can give us what we need. Of course, if anything should happen to Clara before then, I am sure you will regret your decision."

Mrs. Fogbottle gasped, grew red in the face and tried to regain the upper hand. "Well, you are pretty forward for a young woman. I was going to give her the medicine. I am not the kind to be withholding a cure from anyone. Maybe next time, explain what is going on and you will be received with more courtesy." With this curt statement, the big woman stomped from the room to fetch the medicine.

Victoria could barely contain herself from laughing at this display of small-town power being wielded by the two healers in the village.

"A little rivalry between the fort's medicine women," Corporal Greer laughed, "but nothing too serious. Fighting with each other gives them reason to get up in the morning. And thinking about future events, once you have that little girl out of danger, you and Edward are to report to me and give a full briefing on what has been going on. Do you understand, Miss?"

"Yes, Sir. I am sure the medicine will bring Clara around, and we'll be back soon."

Mrs. Fogbottle reappeared with a handful of bottles, dressings and ointments, as well as a soft stuffed toy.

"Give this stuffed toy kitten to Clara when she comes around. Being lost in the woods has likely scared the poor baby, and she'll need something to cuddle to help her forget the nightmare she has been through. May God bring her back to health."

Victoria thanked the austere woman and quickly returned to the cabin.

"Well, it took you long enough," Aunt Violet said. "I would guess the big medicine boss was trying to snatch my little Clara, stow her away in her clinic then ship her away to heaven knows where as soon as my back is turned." She accepted the medicine and immediately gave Clara her first dose of the antibiotic.

"There, child. This may be white man's medicine, but it is one thing I know that is pure magic when it comes to curing infections like yours. Now, sleep and get better my love."

While Clara slept, Victoria recounted her conversation with the tough-minded Mrs. Fogbottle.

"That's a good story. You are better at dealing with that battle-axe than I am. She makes me say things I regret, so I end up turning my back on her and not getting what I need. You will have to forgive me for treating you so badly, Victoria. I misjudged you. You are one of us," Aunt Violet declared.

"We are not that different, Auntie," Edward said. "Mrs. Fogbottle is not all bad. She sounds like a bulldog, but look, she even sent a toy for Clara, so she must have a good heart."

"You think so? I think she was afraid Victoria would tell her father that she was willing to let a little girl from a wood camp die. It wasn't goodness but fear that made her decide to give us the medicine and the gift. Wolverines don't become chipmunks overnight."

"We don't have to go back to see the wolverine, but we must visit the RCMP Office. Corporal Greer ordered Edward and me to make a full report of all the happenings. It looks like Clara is resting peacefully, so maybe we should go now."

"He's a straight shooter, according to my dad," Edward said, as they walked over to the police headquarters.

"Hopefully he'll be able to catch those crooks and help us find Charlie. Where do you think Charlie could be, Edward?"

"Maybe the corporal can shed some light on what has happened since we left Uncle Joe on the Telegraph Trail... what was that, a day or two days ago?"

Chapter XII

The Rock Face

As the day wore on, Charlie's pace slowed even more. His throat was parched, and he was weak from lack of food and water. It was now mid-afternoon, and after a cool morning, the sun beat down through the woods. As he struggled through the willows, he spotted drops of dew nestled in the leaves of pasque flowers. The forest floor was carpeted with the light purple flowers, all holding precious water. He sipped from each leaf he picked, but there was never enough to quench his thirst. Charlie kept his eyes on the ground, careful not to trip as he searched for the tiny flowers. He knew that without water, he might faint and not manage the trek to the river.

At least there is no beaver fever in these pure drops from heaven, he thought, remembering Clara's warning about drinking from small forest streams.

But soon there were no more pasque flowers with the life-giving drops of water. Once more his mouth felt dry, and his lips blistered in the hot sun. Just when Charlie felt he could not go another step without water, he came to a patch of cranberries, bright red in the sunlight and filled with juice. He sat on the ground and grabbed handfuls of the sour fruit, stuffing them in his mouth. Then he leaned back against a flat rock and rested while his body gained strength. He touched the smooth, cool, rock face. He looked up and saw the telegraph wires angling from the trees. Then he saw the cliffs rising up high above him. He was sitting on the edge of the Telegraph Trail and rising up beside him were his Craggy Cliffs. He was out of the forest! He was saved!

"Craggy Cliffs! I found you! The river has to be close by!" The berries had refreshed Charlie, but he needed water. Suddenly, he realized that the Telegraph Trail veered away and that the river was blocked by the ridge of cliffs. He walked along the base of the rock face looking for a way over the steep cliffs.

"I guess the berries were there to give me the strength to climb, and climb I will. I won't give up. I am so close, but if I don't find water, I'll never make it to Fort Selkirk."

Charlie spotted a crack along the face of the rock with small willows and bushes growing up out of it. He moved slowly up the cliff, using the bushes to pull himself up and to keep him from slipping backwards. The last pitch before the top was very steep, but his pack weighed heavily on his back, hindering his climb. He tried several times to climb upward, grabbing onto a willow branch with one hand and pushing against the steep incline with his feet and other hand. The effort exhausted him.

Okay, I guess we will part here. Doesn't look like gold is much good when a person is in real trouble anyway.

Charlie clung to the rock as he opened his pack, carefully lifting out the leather sack of gold.

One nugget for a boat ride and one nugget to get help for Clara, and maybe a little gold dust for a meal for me.

He wrapped the nuggets and the gold dust in a handkerchief then stuffed the leather sack into a crack in the rock. He shrugged his pack on again, which was now so light he hardly noticed it. He reached up once again, found a strong handhold and pulled himself onto the top of the Craggy Cliffs.

Leaving the gold behind had lifted more than the actual weight from his back. He felt free of its burden at last. His sense of relief was doubled when he looked down from the cliff. Across the clearing was the Yukon River. The sight of the blue-green water brought tears to his eyes.

If only you were here with me, Clara. We would be jumping for joy and telling each other what we wanted to eat when we got to safety. "A cabin! And smoke from the chimney! And a boat!"

Now all he had to do was climb down the steep face. Charlie's heart was pounding as he started down the precipice, for as Charlie was keenly aware, going down would be far more difficult than climbing up. On the way up, Charlie could see where to place his hands and could find a route with good footholds. But the rock face was steeper on this side of the cliffs. He made it down a few steps only to climb up again. He searched along the top for a safer route.

He could see the cabin more clearly now. It was not close enough to call for help, but near enough to encourage him to get on with his descent. The comforting view of the cabin was in direct contrast to the bleakness of his position. It was especially frightening for a boy with no energy in reserve, knowing that one faulty step would send him careening down to severe injury or even to his death.

I won't think about that. I can do this.

Charlie peered over the cliff and spotted a line of willows and bush growing in a crack a few feet below where he stood. The crevice was similar to the one he had climbed on the other side, but much smaller, barely the width of his shoe. He was nervous as he turned and faced the cliff. He dangled his feet over the edge before jamming his shoe into the crack. Then he fitted his other foot into the crack while holding firmly onto a thin wedge of rock. His heart pounding, he brought his right hand down and pushed his fist into the crack. His position was so precarious that he was terrified of lifting his other hand off the solid hold at the top.

Charlie knew that if he didn't move soon, he would either have to go back up or risk falling. He let go of the top rock and placed his other hand in the crack. Next, he carefully moved one foot, then the other, then one hand, then the other. Each time he jammed a hand into a crack, the jagged rocks scraped his skin, but the fear that swept over him masked the pain of his bleeding hands. Two more moves, and he was off the steep pitch and into the relative safety of the willows.

Sweat poured from his face as he pulled his foot from the crevice and inched downward. Now the other foot. As he pulled his hand from the crack, more skin tore off his knuckles. Now the other hand, and with the next step he would be able to reach the ledge. He was shaking as he pulled his foot out of the crack. He clung to the rock face, unable to see where the ledge was. Little by little, he lowered his foot. Just before his foot reached the safety of the ledge, his hand slipped out from the crack, and Charlie plummeted down, grasping wildly at the rocks. Sharp rocks cut his arms and chest as he slid across the ledge and down over the steep face.

Charlie flung his arms out on both sides, desperately trying to grab hold of something to stop his fall. He caught a willow, but it slipped from his grasp. He reached again, and this time he got his arm around a good-sized spruce bow and was able to hold fast. Charlie clung to the branch, his heart racing. It was several minutes before he could think clearly enough to assess his situation.

I'm a mess. What would Victoria think of me, all scratched, hanging from a branch over a drop that could kill me? If she were here, I would be all bandaged up. Bandages! At least I kept my first aid kit! Now all I have to do is get off this cliff.

And not far below where he hung, he spotted a route with what looked like sturdy willows for handholds and good footholds all the way to the bottom.

Shaken and exhausted, Charlie made his way down the remaining pitch. He sat down at the base of the cliff and pulled out some bandages to patch up his cuts and scratches.

Now to find water, food and a boat so I can go for help.

Charlie felt relieved. Emotion bubbled up in him, and tears came to his eyes as he walked toward the cabin, imagining all the delicious treats that he would be offered. Even more important to Charlie, however, was that Clara's rescue was at hand.

The walk to the cabin was longer than it had looked from the clifftop. Charlie wanted to run the last few steps, but he could not muster the energy. He stumbled up the steps and knocked.

The door popped open like a cork, and there stood a strange-looking man, dressed in fancy clothes that had gone to ruin. His face was unshaven, and below his eyes were dark sags as big as tea bags. It was not an ugly face. In fact, one could tell this had once been a handsome man, but now, for whatever reason, his dress and expression made him look like a crazy person.

"Well, pardon me," the man said in an oily voice, "but who do I have the pleasure of greeting?" The strange man smiled insincerely as he gave Charlie a slight bow.

"Charlie. My name's Charlie Russell, and I've been lost in the woods for days. I need your help to contact the Mounted Police at Fort Selkirk, so they can search for my friend Clara, who is still lost in the forest."

"Come in then, Master Charlie." He bowed in an overly exaggerated manner. "You are in the domain of Jerome McIntosh, the ruler of these surrounding lands. The only problem with my kingdom is that it is boring out here, and I crave company. It is rewarding to have a bright young man drop in for a visit."

"I'm sorry, but I am not really visiting. I really need your help. I am desperately thirsty, and I haven't eaten for days. Most of all, I *must* find Clara."

"Good gracious, but you are insistent. You knock on my door and expect to be fed without paying and then talk about Clara, whoever she is. I come from an important family, one of the original settlers. Did you know that?"

Charlie was beginning to grasp that he was dealing with someone who had lost his marbles. "All I would like, Sir, is a glass of water, and if you could spare some food, I would be very thankful. I would be happy to pay you. I am actually not feeling that well, having not eaten anything but berries for days."

"Show me your money, and I will think about the food."

Reluctantly, Charlie dug in his pockets and brought out his handkerchief, opened it and held out the two nuggets and the gold dust. There was enough there to pay for hundreds of meals.

"Gold! Now that is strange. Wasn't there someone here asking about gold? Yes, two men came by, looking for a girl and boy and asking if I knew of any gold being found. You would be the boy, am I right? And I guess they would be very interested to know you have some gold on you."

Charlie felt sick at the thought of Red and Zeke being so close on his trail. "When did you see the two men?"

"Let me see." He paused, rubbing his chin. "I remember them, and I think I was supposed to tell them if I saw you, but I forget when that was. Maybe today...or maybe yesterday."

Charlie's heart was in his throat. This couldn't be! Instead of finding someone to help rescue Clara, he could fall into the hands of Red and Zeke. Charlie was becoming increasingly irritated with this strange man. He felt sick, but he thought if he had some food, his headache and queasy stomach would go away.

"Supper. You said that if I gave you some gold, you would give me food and water." Charlie looked about the disheveled cabin in search of food. There was a box of crackers and a few cans on the shelves. "Could I heat up a can of soup and have a few crackers?"

"Hand over the gold and help yourself."

"Here, take the gold dust. I'm keeping the nuggets so I can save Clara."

"You'll have to stoke up the fire, so I'll get you some wood." At that, the strange man disappeared from the cabin.

Charlie felt that paradise had been at hand and then ripped away from him. There would be no help from Jerome McIntosh. Charlie would have to get to the fort and find a rescue party, and he would have to get there fast.

He opened a can of tomato soup and stirred water into the pot. He drank several cups of water and munched on crackers while the soup heated. He had just dished out the soup when he heard several footsteps approaching the house. The door flew open.

Red burst through the room glaring at Charlie. "Okay, where's the gold? Give it up right now, and I won't twist your miserable little neck 'til you choke." Red grabbed the backpack and dumped the contents on the table.

"Where is it, you little thief?" This time it was Zeke who yelled at him. "Give us back our gold, or else you'll be a lot more sorry-looking than you are now."

"Which one of you killed John for the gold?" Charlie asked. "I guess you know I found the gold, so I figure one of you guys killed John."

Red and Zeke were eyeing each other with distrust, like two snakes ready to sink their fangs. Then Red turned to Charlie.

"Nobody coulda found it unless they seed me put it there, so I can't figure out how you got your hands on it."

"You told me that John made off with it," Zeke said in his sullen voice. "So I guess there's another story you'll have to tell the cops if they catch us. I just want my share back." Zeke directed this to Red and then glared at Charlie with his narrow snake-like eyes, as if he was trying to fit a puzzle together but couldn't find the missing pieces.

"What happened to your partner?" Charlie asked with surprising courage. "Did one of you stick a knife in him? Is that how you got the cut on your arm?"

"None of yer business, you sneaky brat." Red grabbed Charlie's arm and started to squeeze.

"Ouch! Let me go, you bully."

Zeke was on one flank and Jerome on the other. "We agreed, no hurting the kid," Zeke said. "We need him alive, so he can tell us where the gold is." Red would have continued roughing up Charlie had Jerome not stepped in as well, with even fewer unselfish reasons.

"There will be no such goings-on in my house. I come from respectable people, though I may be down and out for the moment." His voice was as smooth and slick as fat drippings. "For a price, I will take all of you downriver to Fort Selkirk. If the boy stole the gold, then the corporal will see to his punishment."

"I don't want to go with these men because they mean to hurt me. One of them is lying about the gold, and I think one of them is a murderer."

"That may be, young Master Charlie, but they have given me a gold nugget to take them to Fort Selkirk, and I have only a bit of gold dust from you."

"Give us back our gold. Empty your pockets, boy," Red ordered.

Charlie reached in his pocket and held out the gold nugget towards Red, then with a feint, quickly passed it to Jerome. "My passage money. If I have to go with these two crooks, I will pay you to see that I am delivered safely to Fort Selkirk. Protect me from these thugs, and there will be more where this came from. Since I will be informing the RCMP about you two, I suggest you both stay here and find a rock to crawl under."

"Eventually, you will go back for the gold, and when you do, I'll be right behind you," threatened Red. "Besides, the police got nothin' on us. Just a bunch of kids makin' up stories. Dat's all."

Jerome fingered the gold nugget, looking pleased at his sudden good fortune. There in his hand was enough money to buy a passage back to his family's home in Toronto, enough money to make them believe he had hit it rich, enough to make them believe he was a success after all.

"I am grateful for your fares but ask that you keep your differences with the boy to yourselves. Don't know that it is right to be after a kid, and the captain's boy at that. If my bread is buttered and you keep me out of any dirty business, I can keep my mouth shut, providing there is a little more of the shiny stuff coming my way. What do you say to fifty percent of the gold? Nothing illegal, now. I don't hold with that. My family would take me out of their will if I was ever to be on the wrong side of the law. Good family, you know. The best."

Charlie wanted to tell the puffed-up Jerome that even if he were related to the King of England himself, it would mean precious little. It was obvious from his actions that not much moral fiber was passed down from the early founders of Canada, at least, not in his case. If Charlie ended up with his throat slit, Jerome would turn his head and then come back to pick up any booty that happened to fall his way. However, Jerome's lack of principle also protected Charlie. Red and Zeke were quite aware that if they harmed Charlie, Jerome would blackmail them for a good portion of the gold. This understanding created an uneasy truce among the three men.

Now I am in with two crooks, one of them likely a murderer, plus a scheming underhanded scoundrel.

Charlie held his tongue, knowing that he had to depend on Jerome to take him to Fort Selkirk and to control Red's violent impulses. It wasn't long before the three men and the boy were loaded in the boat and on their way. It would be a miserable boat ride for Charlie. He felt like throwing up as soon as they were on the water.

Chapter XIII

The Royal Canadian Mounted Police

Victoria and Edward went to the RCMP building to be interviewed. It was a substantial log structure in the middle of the village. They knocked and were greeted with a smile by the tall, imposing corporal.

"Now, Edward and Victoria, tell me the whole story from A to Z," Corporal Greer instructed.

"First, Sir, please tell me what you know about my brother's whereabouts. You said that Uncle Joe didn't find him. So where is he?"

"It isn't as bad as you think. Joe tracked him to Crazy Jerome's cabin and sent word upriver with Squinteye who was coming to the fort by boat. Joe told Squinteye that he found no one at Jerome's cabin and no boat. Where else can they all be going? So, I calculate the boy is likely on his way to the fort and that we should expect him here. I've been checking the boats arriving, but so far, there's been no sign of him. I suggest you take turns watching the docks, and no doubt, he will turn up."

"Who is that guy, and why is he called Crazy Jerome? Is my brother in his clutches now?" Victoria asked.

"Jerome is not playing with a full deck, but so far he has stayed on the right side of the law. He was an embarrassment to his family, so they gave him enough money to come north and make his own way in life. Being at the bottom of the social ladder of the Yukon has been humiliating for him, and he has more or less lost his marbles. But let's get on with your story." The corporal picked up his notepad and took careful notes while Edward and Victoria explained everything that had happened since the S.S. *Klondike* landed at the Echo Valley wood camp.

Edward felt that Red was the villain and that he had possibly murdered the third partner, but he wasn't sure because no one had found the body or the gold. Victoria felt that Zeke had stolen the gold and killed their partner.

"I thought they were telling the truth when we first met up with Red and Zeke. Now I'm confused. What puzzles me the most is why they're chasing my brother and Clara."

"Had it occurred to you that maybe one of the children found the gold? Is there anything you can remember to indicate that?"

"Victoria, remember Charlie acting strangely on the way back from the trapping cabin? He went into the woods and came back holding something in his jacket."

"Then he clammed up and said nothing for the next day. But I still can't believe he would keep something as important as that from me. I have looked after him since he was little." Victoria's voice choked. "He used to drive me nuts most of the time, but now I would do anything to find him safe and sound."

"Let's wait the night out. By morning, your brother should get here. If not, we will launch a search party and ask your Uncle Joe to help.

"Joe is one remarkable tracker. Last year, he found that scoundrel who killed a customer over a remark about the cooking. Remember that one? Everyone called him the Bacon and Egg Killer. Cooked at the roadhouse upriver, where was that…at…Green Valley, I think. Well this traveller stopped for the night and was given his breakfast. I guess the eggs were overcooked, and he told the cook he wasn't going to pay good money to eat eggs that tasted like leather. Well, the cook went to the kitchen, came back with a butcher knife and stuck it into the traveller's chest. Before anyone else at the roadhouse could stop him, the Bacon and Egg Killer took off into the bush. Your uncle started tracking him the next day, never lost his trail. In ten days, he cornered him and brought him to justice.

"Good tracker, that man,…the best." Corporal Greer obviously enjoyed being a storyteller as much as he enjoyed being an officer of the law.

"So you two should check the dock. Seems to me your brother will get here somehow. Oh, and tell your aunt that trouble is brewing in the form of Mrs. Fogbottle, who has been on the blower trying to get a bigwig in Whitehorse to order your aunt to bring Clara to the clinic. I know that won't go down well, but the Superintendent for Indian Affairs in Whitehorse has the power to do just that. If he tells me to bring her under the care of Mrs. Fogbottle, bring her I will. But I'm sorry if I have to do that. Just a warning. I like to have peace in the community, but with those two at each other's throats, war will continue to rage until one of them departs Fort Selkirk."

"My auntie will not let Clara go. Not without a battle."

"It won't come to that. I will reason with your aunt. She and I get along just fine. Hopefully you will help me by talking to your aunt, should the missus get her way. Speaking of the power in the community, look who's approaching."

The stern matron burst through the door, waving a telegram. "Corporal, your orders." With a haughty glance at Victoria, she placed the paper in the corporal's hands. "I'll come with you just to make sure the child is properly cared for as we move her to the clinic."

"No need for that, Mrs. Fogbottle. I will speak with Violet. Victoria and Edward, would you back me up on this? My hands are tied, and I don't want Clara to be upset."

They walked silently across the grassy expanse to Violet's little cabin. No one looked forward to taking the brunt of Violet's bad temper when she learned that Mrs. Fogbottle had gotten her way.

As the boat powered towards Fort Selkirk, Charlie felt increasingly ill. He thought the soup and crackers would have made him feel better, but he had stomach cramps as if he were being attacked from inside.

Sweat poured down his cheeks and he burned with a fever. Suddenly, his stomach heaved, and he vomited uncontrollably over the side of the boat. Another cramp hit his stomach, and he retched again, this time only throwing up bile.

After that, he lay on the bottom of the boat moaning, "Oh boy, am I sick!"

"Here, take a bit of water to settle your stomach." It was Zeke who had come to his aid. The thin man with the shifty eyes was not Charlie's idea of a comforting nurse, but Charlie's throat was raw, so he lifted his head a little to take a sip. He sloshed the water in his mouth to get rid of the foul taste and then spit out over the side of the boat. Then he took a long drink, which did little to make him feel better.

"Leave him be," Red ordered. "He's just getting seasick. And to think he's the son of a riverboat captain. If he didn't look like the sorriest sight in the world, I would think he was just putting this on to keep us from asking him where he hid the gold."

Charlie knew this was not seasickness. He had been on the river with his dad ever since he was a toddler and had never been sick.

Clara was awake and taking spoonsful of soup from her aunt. The colour was back in her cheeks.

"Hi, Victoria," Clara called from her bed. "Auntie Violet said you were going to find out about Charlie. Did Uncle Joe find him? I bet he did."

"Not yet, but don't worry. The corporal is certain he is heading for the fort and that we will all be together soon."

At this point, Aunt Violet noticed the corporal. "And I suppose that witch from the clinic has used her evil power and is going to take my niece?"

"Now, now, Violet, she doesn't mean any harm. Clara will have everything she needs at the clinic, and you can come sit by her side anytime you want. But yes, she did manage to get the authorities to order me to move the child. Because the parents are away, Clara becomes a ward of Canada. There is nothing I can do but follow orders, although it does make me sad to enforce the law in this case. I have nothing but the highest regard for your nursing skills."

"Thank you very much, but I don't need the butter slabbed on quite that thick. You're the law, and you're telling me to let my little niece go off into the care of that woman."

"Auntie, I think you should just go along with the corporal. He has to take Clara no matter what we say. I don't want Clara to be upset. Let's tell her it will be great to go to the clinic, that there are books and toys there, and that one of us will always be with her." Edward spoke in a whisper so that Clara didn't hear.

"Hmmph. All I can say is it's a good thing You Know Who didn't come here. I would never willingly put my niece into her care. But if I am welcome in the clinic and can still bring spruce tea for her fever and use my poultice for her injured arm, then I won't put up a fight. But this won't be the last Mrs. Fogbottle hears from me."

With those words, Violet bustled about, packing herbs, tucking a blanket about Clara and placing the fluffy toy in the little girl's arms. Edward carried his sister and followed the corporal over to the clinic with Violet and Victoria trailing behind.

Clara settled happily into the clinic, feeling more and more chipper with each passing hour. She recounted her frightening journey through the forest and the events that led up to becoming separated from Charlie.

"I know Charlie is feeling bad about leaving me. I am sure he didn't mean to call me names or leave me behind. It was early morning, and we were so cold and cranky. I guess he got mad at me for always telling him what I had learned in school. Don't be angry at him, please."

"If he comes back safely, I will only feel relief," Victoria said. "And now that I think about it, you should be sleeping. I will take one more walk down to the river to see if any boats are arriving. Sleep well, Clara. Edward will stay with you, won't you?"

"I'll be right here. Just call if you need me, Sis."

Chapter XIV

Beaver Fever

The cramps in Charlie's stomach subsided, allowing him to sleep until the bumping of the boat against the dock at Fort Selkirk jolted him awake. It was dark now, and quiet once the motor was switched off. Charlie realized he had to escape these men if he was to get help for Clara. He staggered to his feet, ducked under Red's arms and hopped out the side of the boat. His legs were weak and after a few steps up the steep bank, Red grabbed him in a tight arm lock.

"Don't try any funny stuff, kid. You got nothin' on us. I knows you stashed the gold, and before the night is over, yer gonna take me to it."

"I...you're hurting me. Let go!"

The big man put his hands around Charlie's neck and started to squeeze. "This is what I will do to your sister and your little friend if you don't hand over the gold. Got me, kid?"

Just then, Victoria appeared at the top of the bank. In the dark, all Red could see was a black shape against the sky. Red released his grip on Charlie. The boy staggered a few steps, felt his head spin and passed out. Red and Zeke ran up the bank, away from any watching eyes. Jerome, not wanting anyone to think he was part of a plan to hurt Charlie, quickly took the boat out into the river and headed back to his cabin. He had the gold nuggets in his pocket. Life would be different now.

Victoria ran down the bank and bent over her brother's unconscious body. "Charlie! Are you okay? Oh, my goodness! Charlie, can you hear me? It's Victoria."

Charlie mumbled, "Clara! I need to find Clara." He immediately passed out again.

"Charlie! Oh dear!" Victoria knew she couldn't carry her brother up the steep slope. She placed her sweater over him and ran to get Edward. In a few minutes, the tall teenager had scooped Charlie off the ground and was carrying him to the clinic.

"Could you run and get Aunt Violet?" Edward asked. "We'll need both medicine women if we are to save Charlie."

Victoria ran across the grassy yard to Violet's cabin and explained that her brother had been found but was very ill.

"You say he fainted and was talking gibberish. I will go right over and see what can be done. Hmm, he likely has had nothing to eat for days. Maybe he is just weak from lack of food."

She was out the door, still muttering about various illnesses she may have to deal with. Victoria followed Violet to the clinic, where Mrs. Fogbottle presided.

The professional nurse and the Indigenous healer hovered over the sick boy, assessing his vital signs and trying to decide what was making him sick.

"I think he is starving and needs some chicken soup," Mrs. Fogbottle asserted. "I always think chicken soup works."

"If he is starving, why has he been vomiting? And he stinks like rotten eggs. Besides, his skin is the colour of an old sheet. I don't mean to say you are not good at figuring out what is wrong with someone, but I would say it is not lack of food. I think he has some illness."

"And what nursing school did you graduate from to be telling me about illnesses?"

Edward and Victoria listened to this battle between the two Titans over who was the better healer.

Clara woke up. She was delighted that Charlie was out of the forest. She listened but felt sure Charlie would recover under the care of the two competent women even though they argued nonstop. She wanted to tell them to give him some of Violet's tea and a little of Mrs. Fogbottle's chicken soup when she remembered something that happened when she and Charlie were lost in the forest.

"Auntie Violet. What are his symptoms, please?"

"Every few minutes he has bad stomach cramps. He is flatulent, and he has no colour."

"Flatulent? Are those smelly farts?" Clara asked.

"Well, we don't use such crude words," Mrs. Fogbottle answered haughtily, "but yes, very smelly."

Clara was quiet for a minute then whispered to her brother. "Edward, remember the medical book I had, the one I used to read when I was bored in the winter. I read about those symptoms, and I think I may know what is wrong with Charlie."

"It's going to be a shock to them if a ten-year-old is able to figure out what is wrong with Charlie, so break it to them gently."

"Auntie Violet, did you think about what would happen if Charlie had been drinking from a stream in the forest, downstream from a beaver dam?"

"Giardia!" both women said at once.

"Luckily, I have penicillin, the perfect medicine for giardia." Mrs. Fogbottle headed off to her well-stocked medicine cupboard like a steamboat under power, while Violet rifled through her bottles and baskets of dried herbs.

"I have no objection to the medicine you have stored in your cupboard. I do not have the correct herb right now." Auntie Violet said. "I will admit your medicines are an excellent cure for giardia, but of course it is likely a cure long known to my people. Likely stolen from us and copied. Quick, let's give him a dose and then a little spruce tea."

Charlie sipped a little of Violet's tea along with the medicine and mumbled something about Clara that they couldn't understand.

"Now go to sleep, Charles," Mrs. Fogbottle said, "and we'll give you some chicken soup when you wake."

"No!" Charlie cried, deliriously. "I can't sleep. Clara is lost. It's my fault. I argued with her. I was really mean to her." Charlie sobbed as he poured out all the guilt he had been harbouring for the past three days. "Get the police, please! They need to find her right away, or she'll die."

"She's right here, child," Violet assured the tortured boy.

"No, she's lost in the forest! I have to go with them and help find her. Please," he begged

Clara walked over to Charlie's bed. "I'm here, Charlie."

"You can't be here. I left you in the forest all alone," Charlie cried out in his delirium.

"I'm right here by your bed."

"I am afraid to believe that because when I was lost, I saw things, and then they disappeared. I can't believe you are really here."

"See, I am real." Clara touched Charlie's cheek with her fingertips. It felt like a kiss to Charlie. He smiled at Clara, and an enormous weight lifted from his chest.

"How did you get out of the woods?" Charlie was all smiles, despite his weakened condition.

"Uncle Joe found me, and I am safe and sound. My auntie looked after me just like she'll look after you."

"Get back to bed, child," Mrs. Fogbottle said to Clara.

"Yes, dear, go back to your bed," Violet added in her soft voice. "Charlie needs to rest. Tomorrow, the two of you can exchange stories all day."

Charlie, relieved of the worry over Clara, fell asleep immediately and didn't wake up again until late the next morning. He had recovered and was ravenous. Clara's injury was healing, and for the first time since her rescue, she had an appetite.

Violet and Mrs. Fogbottle competed with one another to win approval from Clara and Charlie for their cooking. There were sausages and eggs from the kitchen clinic, and bannock and canned berries from Violet's house. Charlie and Clara told of their journey together and how they had come to be separated. Charlie was about to explain his theory of the gold and who the real criminal was when Violet interrupted them.

"Victoria, I need some more comfrey. Would you run over to my cabin and bring the basket where I store the herbs? Clara's arm is still inflamed, and there is nothing better than comfrey to fix that and to ease the pain."

Victoria did not want to miss the next part of the story, but she did not hesitate to do as Aunt Violet asked. "Don't say another word, Charlie, until I get back. I need to know what Zeke did to you, and everything about Red and Crazy Jerome."

Victoria rushed to Violet's cabin, hurried about the kitchen and located the neatly labeled birch bark basket. Suddenly, the door swung open. She gasped at the sight of Zeke, his bearded face and shifty gaze more frightening to her now that she was alone with him.

"If you don't come willingly, I'll take you anyway." Zeke raised a pistol, pointing it at Victoria's head. "I'll use this if you give me any trouble. I don't want to hurt you, so do as I say."

Victoria was so frightened, she was unable to scream for help.

"Don't make a sound, and put your hands behind your back." Victoria's heart raced as Zeke tied her hands and wrapped a kerchief tightly across her mouth. He took a note from his pocket and placed it on the kitchen table.

Zeke pulled and pushed Victoria out the back door and through the woods, skirting behind the buildings and then down to the dock. Red was waiting for them in a stolen boat.

"Good work, Zeke! Git her in before someone spots us."

Zeke dragged the girl into the boat, and Red pushed them away from the dock.

"I've just about had enough with youse kids telling the cops we murdered John," Red growled. "Now we're on the run, but I am going to git our gold back, and I know jest how I will git it back. Youse is comin' with us, and then we will see if your little brother still holds out on me."

Chapter XV

Showdown at Craggy Cliffs

"Where could that girl be? I can't figure out why she's taking so long." Violet shook her head. "Edward, go see what's keeping Victoria."

Edward was also perplexed that Victoria would not have rushed back to hear the remainder of Charlie's story.

Charlie, now with his fill of food and relieved that Clara was safe, dozed off again. Mrs. Fogbottle had just given Clara an aspirin for pain and another dose of antibiotic when Edward burst through the door. He held a note in his hand and gave it to Violet with a look of anguish.

"Shush, Edward. Let's go into the kitchen to discuss this."

"What's going on here?" Mrs. Fogbottle demanded, holding out her hand for the note.

"Oh, no! Not Victoria!" Mrs. Fogbottle exclaimed. "Edward, take this to the corporal. He'll deal with this."

"But it says that if we involve the police, we will never see Victoria again. We're to bring the gold to Jerome's cabin by midnight, if Charlie wants to see his sister again."

"This isn't a matter for children to deal with. Now, do as I say."

"You tell Corporal Greer if you must. I'm going to ask Charlie if he knows where the gold is. Then I am going to find Victoria."

"You will do no such thing, young man." Mrs. Fogbottle placed her hands on her hips. "I won't have you upsetting young Charles. He is not well enough yet."

"He will be far worse if something happens to Victoria, and he discovers I did not do everything possible to rescue her. Sorry, Ma'am, but you can go see the corporal. I will be checking in with Charlie and getting his side of the story."

Edward woke Charlie, who surfaced from a deep sleep. "You need to find Clara," he said in a dazed voice.

"Clara is napping and is safe. It's your sister." Edward read the note out loud, and it didn't take Charlie long to realize the danger Victoria faced. He remembered Red's threat: *This is what I will do to your sister unless I git the gold.*

He explained to Edward that he still didn't know if Zeke or Red was a murderer or even if their partner had been murdered at all. He also gave Edward a detailed account of the malicious Crazy Jerome. "He won't actually put the knife into your back, but he might help someone else as long as he has some gold to grease his palm."

"I'll be careful with all three of them until I find out exactly how the gold ended up in the woods where you picked it up. Now, tell me where you hid the gold. I have to take it to them by midnight, or else they may harm Victoria."

Charlie tried to explain where he'd cached the gold, but realized that it would be impossible for Edward to find the crevice and then locate the sack of gold which he had stuffed well down into the crack in the rock.

"Edward, I have to go with you. You won't find the gold on your own. Honest, except for being hungry, I feel fine. I have to come. Please don't say no."

"Mrs. Fogbottle will have me put in jail if I take you along with me."

"They won't know you agreed to take me. I'll leave a note telling them it was totally my idea to go, that you insisted I stay but I snuck out when you weren't looking."

"I hope I won't regret this, but I guess you should come not just to show me where you hid the gold, but also for another reason."

"What's that?"

"I'm afraid of heights and could no more climb that cliff by myself than fly to the moon. So, meet me at the dock in a couple of minutes. I am going over to Auntie's for supplies."

"Bring a mirror, paper and pen, and if I have to go up that steep cliff again, I will need a backpack and rope. And food. Bring lots of food."

Violet reluctantly helped Edward with a few supplies. "You should wait for your Uncle Joe to get here and go with him and the corporal. And don't bother that boy. He needs his rest. And why are you taking so much food, Edward?" Violet lectured as she gathered up the items and then gave her nephew a hug, cautioning him to be very careful and come back safely.

Edward ran to the dock where he had moored the boat. Charlie was already there.

"What did you bring to eat?" Charlie asked.

"Not to worry, Charlie. We have dried meat, a chunk of cheese, several pieces of bannock, jam, butter and a piece of the cake Mrs. Fogbottle left unattended in her kitchen. Will that last you for the trip downriver to Jerome's, or should I make another foray to the store and buy a sack of groceries?"

"Thanks, Ed. That sounds great. Pass the bag to me, and I will munch along the way."

"Before stuffing your mouth, how about untying the rope so we can get out of here before Mrs. Fogbottle alerts the town and sends the corporal after us?"

It was late afternoon when they finally approached Jerome's cabin. Edward cut the motor, landing at a spot hidden in the trees and away from the cabin. They covered the boat with willows and crept onto the bank, keeping out of sight and approaching the cabin through the dense willows and underbrush.

"I want to take a look inside, Ed. Can we get closer?"

"I should go alone. Two people make more noise. You stay here while I have a look inside the cabin to see if I can spot your sister. I've spent enough time in the bush with Uncle Joe, and I've learned how to move quietly through the woods without alerting everyone within earshot."

"I agree. I'm more the crash-and-burn type. But take that mirror. Use it to look in the window just in case someone happens to be staring out when you stick your mug up to the glass."

"That's why you asked me to bring a mirror. I wondered. You're a real Sherlock Holmes, Chuck. Okay, here I go."

Charlie remained in the woods while Edward crept slowly and quietly to the back window of the cabin. Charlie was so tense that he was barely breathing as he watched his friend. Soon Edward was directly under the window. He positioned the mirror up to the glass, turning first one way, then another, and held it there for what seemed like much too long to Charlie. Edward crept back to Charlie, moving silently through the bush.

"Did you see Victoria? Is she all right?"

"She's sitting on a chair, not tied up. She seems unharmed, but she looks scared."

"Who's with her?"

"All three of them are there, sitting around the table 'chewing the fat'. It looks like none of them like or trust each other much. I could hear Red giving them a piece of his mind, telling Zeke that he's useless and that Jerome could go back to his stuffy, rich relatives and ask them for money rather than expect to cash in on the gold. Then Zeke starts up, accusing Red of killing John and saying that he would hang for it."

"What do we do now? Go see them and bargain?"

"I don't know. What would your hero, the great Sherlock Holmes, do?

"I don't trust Red. He would slit our throats, dump us in the river and think nothing of it. Zeke, I don't know. Sometimes I think he is the shiftiest thug I have ever met, but then he seems to have a human side, too. It's as if there are two people battling inside his brain. Better watch out for Jerome, though, he is the unknown...crazy is right."

"So, we can't knock on the door, or they may capture us and threaten to kill Victoria unless you show them where the gold is," Edward said. "Once they have the gold, our lives are worthless. We need to get ourselves into a better bargaining position. If you get the gold and show them that you have it in your hands, do you think we could force them into freeing Victoria? If they have a choice of the money or Victoria, they will definitely choose the gold. After all, the reason they kidnapped your sister was to force you to give up the gold."

"But we know that if they let us go," Charlie added, "we have enough evidence to put them in the clink even if the police never prove that they murdered John. We are the only witnesses to their crimes, although whether there was a murder remains a mystery. So, they won't want us ratting them out to the police."

"So, we agree," Edward summed up. "We need to get the upper hand. I have a plan. I'm glad you asked me to bring something to write with. Tell me what you think of this." He handed a note to Charlie.

We have the gold at the foot of the cliffs near Jerome's house. Come in twenty minutes, and bring Victoria. When you free her, we will hand over the gold.

"I'll take the note and slip it through the door. By the time they see it, I'll be gone."

Charlie watched as Edward crept up to the cabin door. It was like watching a shadow. The Indigenous boy moved quietly through the woods and slipped the note under the door, knocked and as smooth and light as a cat, returned to where Charlie crouched behind the bushes.

The two boys then moved quietly through the woods and, when they were out of sight of the cabin, they ran to the foot of Charlie's Craggy Cliffs.

"Can you climb up there on your own, Chuck? Climbing is not my thing."

"I think I know how to do this better now." He put on his backpack, took the rope from Edward and draped it around his shoulders. He started the ascent of the crevice and soon reached the steep pitch near the top. This time he felt stronger and more confident. He dug his feet into the cracks and pulled himself over the top.

He waved to Edward, who gave a sign to Charlie and hid in the bushes. Charlie saw the three men leaving the cabin with Victoria. He felt a stab of pain in his chest at seeing his sister in the clutches of those dangerous men.

He watched for a minute. Zeke was holding Victoria's arm. She pulled free and walked beside Red, as if she would be safer with the big man than with Zeke.

Wow, Victoria must still think that Red is innocent and that Zeke is the murderer!

Jerome, the lesser-known factor among these men, followed the two miners.

His mind must be as busy as a conniving wolverine, Charlie thought, *likely trying to figure out a way of getting a good share of the gold without having the law after him.*

Charlie was aware that his actions in the next few minutes were crucial for his sister. He tried to calm his nerves as he tied the rope firmly around a rock on the other side of the cliffs. He held onto the rope as he let himself down.

Hey, this is easy! he thought. *Just lean out, hold the rope and walk down the pitch, just like Buck Rogers did in the book when he landed on that planet. I forget what the rock climbers call this. I'll ask Clara. She knows just about every word in the dictionary.*

In minutes, he was off the steep pitch and digging the sack of gold out of the crack in the rock. With the gold safely in his pack, he held onto the rope and easily scaled to the top of the Craggy Cliffs. Charlie removed the rope and walked to the lookout. He saw the three men and his sister at the foot of the cliffs.

"Charlie!" Victoria yelled. "Please be careful."

Just like my sister. Always telling me what to do.

But this time, Charlie felt no resentment. The concern his sister expressed made him realize how much Victoria cared for him and how very much he wanted to save her.

"Kid!" Red yelled. "Did you git the gold?'

Charlie took his pack off and held the sack up for Red to see.

Jerome, believing everyone to be dishonest, whispered to Red who nodded and called out to Charlie. "Show me there is gold in that there sack and not just rocks."

Charlie picked out a couple of nuggets and held them up. Gold chunks glinted in the glow of the sunset.

"Throw it down, and I will let her go," the big red-haired man yelled.

"Let Victoria go, and then I'll throw it down," Charlie replied. At this point, Edward stepped out from the bushes.

"Victoria is to walk slowly towards me. Charlie will throw the sack down when she is halfway here." Edward's voice sounded calm and firm, but his heart was pounding.

"I'll git the gold from youse kids!" Red yelled. He shoved Victoria over to Zeke. "Don't let her go, ya hear? Give me the gold, kid! I don't want youse kids rattin' on me to the cops. Jerome, you catch the other boy, and if you let 'im escape, I'll make sure you join Zeke and me in jail."

"Half the gold," Jerome replied, "and I'll catch the youngster."

"One third is all youse is gitting." Red was already part-way up the cliff.

"Okay one-third." Jerome drew a gun and walked towards Edward, weapon raised. But the teen held his ground. Jerome was a sleaze, Edward decided, but he had not sunk to the level of murdering children or, more likely, he did not have the guts to actually pull the trigger.

Victoria shrieked in terror at being left with Zeke. Despite her screams, Zeke kept a tight grip on her wrist.

The first pitch was easy for the big man, and soon he was at the steep section near the top. Charlie didn't know what to do, should Red catch him before Victoria was freed.

"I won't give you the gold until you set Victoria free."

"Youse won't have anything to say about it, 'cause when I catch you, I'll cook your goose. Youse will also tell me how you found the gold when it was hid under a pile of rocks. No one could have found it unless they seed me put it there."

"You must be dumb as a sack of hammers if you don't even remember where you hid the gold. I found it under a log."

"It weren't under any log!" Red screamed out. "It was under a pile of rocks, a big pile of rocks!"

Charlie looked surprised at this and mumbled to himself, "Hidden under a rock pile?" Then, it hit him and Red at the same time!

It was Zeke who'd hidden the gold under the log and, thought Charlie. *If Zeke hid the gold, maybe he killed John, too.*

Charlie was confused. "I'm coming down!" he yelled.

He ran along the top of the cliff to the steepest pitch. He looped the rope about a rocky outcrop and swung himself over the edge. With giant leaps, Charlie bounced down the cliff, landing a short distance from where Zeke held Victoria. Then, realizing that Red could use the rope as well, Charlie pulled on one end to release the rope, but it snagged on a jagged rock. Charlie flipped the rope several times trying to free it. Red had gained the top of the cliff and was racing to grab the rope before Charlie could recover it. The big man lunged and caught the end of the rope.

"Ed, help me!"

Edward ran to join Charlie.

"On the count of three, pull! One. Two. Three!" Edward yelled, and they yanked the rope from Red's grasp.

"Victoria! We have to save her." Charlie looked at his sister, still firmly in Zeke's grasp.

"We're ready to trade," Edward announced, trying to sound calm. "Zeke, let Victoria go. When she is safely beside us, Charlie will throw the gold to you."

Red stomped across the top of the cliff, looking for a safe route down. "Zeke, hold onto the girl until you have the gold in your hands," Red yelled. "Once we have the gold, we'll take care of these brats. Then we disappear into the bush. The law ain't never gonna find us."

Zeke released Victoria, who ran towards the boys, tears of relief streaming down her cheeks. Just before Victoria reached Charlie, he tossed the sack of gold. It landed between Jerome and Zeke.

"Thank you, my brave little brother." She hugged Charlie so tightly he could barely breathe, and then she put her arms around Edward, kissing him lightly on the cheek. "Thank you for saving me."

Jerome quickly grabbed the sack. His fist firmly clutching the gold, he slowly backed towards his cabin, still pointing the gun at Zeke. Feeling the weight of the gold—thousands of dollars to restore his position in society—a grin spread across his face.

"Oh no, you don't!" It was Red, climbing down the last section of the crevice. He was directly above Jerome. The big man heaved himself from the cliff, knocking Jerome to the ground. The two men scuffled, and the sack fell from Jerome's hand.

Zeke realized that he would soon be entirely out of the spoils once Red was finished with Jerome. He grabbed the sack as the other two men wrestled in the dirt.

"Let's head for the boat!" Charlie yelled. "Let them kill each other over the gold! It only brought me trouble."

The three children ran to the river and jumped in the boat. The motor roared into action, and Edward pointed the boat towards Fort Selkirk. They were on the water for only a minute before they heard the sound of another motorboat.

"They're chasing us!" Victoria screamed.

Edward turned the boat, spraying water as he banked into a sharp circle, heading away from the approaching vessel.

"Gun it, Edward! They're gaining on us." Charlie's voice was almost a whisper. He was terrified at the prospect of being caught by the villains once more.

Edward opened up the throttle, but the boat did not surge ahead. Instead, the motor sputtered and died.

"We're cooked!" Charlie said. "What do we do now?"

"Think of something, quick!" Victoria was frantic.

"Nah, I think we will be just fine," Edward said, smiling at his friends.

"You're as crazy as Jerome!" Charlie said.

"See for yourself."

Victoria and Charlie turned to watch the big boat approach.

"Hey! It's your uncle and Corporal Greer. How 'bout that?" Charlie giggled, feeling the same relief he had experienced after escaping the teeth of the grizzly.

The next day, a feast was laid out in the Savoie Hotel at Fort Selkirk. The S.S. *Klondike* was docked at the river, and Captain Russell, Mr. MacTavish, the RCMP officers, Mrs. Fogbottle, Aunt Violet and Uncle Joe all gathered to celebrate with the four children. Not that they agreed with the risks the children had taken. There had been a lengthy scolding from the adults: *You should have known better than to take the law into your own hands! Why in the world would you pick up the sack of gold and then not report it to the police immediately? What were you thinking when you ran off with Edward to rescue Victoria?*

The children answered politely, trying to explain that they were only doing what they thought was right at the time, and that, yes, they agreed that they would never, ever take such risks again. They all enjoyed a fine dinner of moose meat, fresh vegetables grown in the Fort Selkirk gardens, and wild blueberry pies. Then it was time for everyone to reveal what they knew about the criminals, and what had transpired between the unfortunate John and his two criminal partners.

"I found John's body near the trail to your trapping cabin," Uncle Joe explained to the group. "Looks like quite a struggle took place. I left him where he lay because I knew the corporal would not want me tampering with the evidence." He paused for a minute till everyone around the table gave him their full attention. "I walked back up the trail to the trapline cabin. They obviously cleared the cupboards bare except for cereal and beans. My guess is they took all the canned food and the bacon. I could see by the tracks, that although John McAllister had been there earlier, he wasn't the one who stole your food. It was Red and Zeke."

"So, they *were* the ones who vandalized our cabin?" Edward concluded.

"From what I could gather from Red and Zeke, who, by the way, are safely in jail, John wanted to leave some gold to pay for the food they ate. That is what started an argument and led Red to steal the gold."

"I wouldn't be able to charge anyone with murder, had it not been for Uncle Joe finding the body of the unfortunate John McAllister. Before Victoria was kidnapped, Uncle Joe took me to the crime scene," Corporal Greer explained.

"Did Zeke kill him?" Charlie asked.

"They've each accused the other of the murder. We'll charge Red and Zeke with kidnapping and theft, and Red will likely hang for the brutal murder of John McAllister," Corporal Greer said. "Joe could see by the big boot tracks that it was Red who killed John McAllister."

"But Red said he stashed the gold under a pile of rocks. but I found it under a log. So, I figured that Zeke hid the gold under the log and murdered John," Charlie said.

"It was the tracks that told the story," Uncle Joe explained. "The men stayed in your cabin the night before you met them. Red was still furious with John for insisting that they leave some gold to pay for the use of the cabin and their supper. Looks to me like Red tried to sneak off during the night, and John became suspicious and followed him. There was a fight, and Red killed John with a knife then hid the body. Zeke didn't see Red kill John, but he woke up in time to see Red hide the gold under the rock pile. Zeke carried the gold down the trail a ways and hid it under the log where you found it, Charlie."

Captain Greer took up the story. "I was able to get a confession from Red because of the evidence. The tracks told the story. I thank Joe for that." He stood up and raised his glass to Joe. "Best tracker in the Yukon."

"What about Jerome?" Charlie asked.

"He will be charged with kidnapping and assault, although he continues to argue that no one in his family would ever do anything against the law. When I told him I had sent a telegram informing his family that he was in jail, he wailed like a baby."

"What about the gold?" Clara asked. "Will Charlie get to keep it?"

"It will go to John's wife Sara," Captain Russell said, finally entering the conversation. "She lives in Dawson City with their four-year-old twins, a boy and girl—beautiful children. Sara brought some flowers to your mother before the news of John's death reached her. Your mom is doing well now, Clara, and I imagine she will be comforting Sara."

"You also met up again with Lord Littleheart?" Mr. McIntosh remarked.

"Oh, yes!" Captain Russell got up from the table and opened a big box. "He sent presents. He regrets the accident that put Mrs. McIntosh in the hospital and hopes his gifts will, in some small way, redeem him. A dress for Clara; pants, shirt and shoes for Edward; and for Charlie a pair of long denim pants."

"What about my mother?" Clara asked. "She was the one who was hurt."

"Why, yes. He gave your mother a brand-new sewing machine, your father a Winchester rifle and, for me, fishing gear so I could take my son to Swan Lake and catch that thirty-pound trout."

"What about me?" Victoria asked, feeling left out.

"Littlehart will send you a copy of his book once he returns to England and gets it published. Right now, he is living with Billy's family and working the placer mine."

"Billy's family. Really?" Victoria exclaimed. "That must be a big change for someone used to living in a castle with servants. Are you sure?"

"Victoria thought Billy wasn't good enough to play with me because he had to travel in second class. I guess you were wrong, Victoria," Charlie said, "and I guess Littlehart is smarter than I gave him credit for."

"People do change for the good, and sometimes they admit they're wrong," Victoria said, with a smile, thinking that she had learned a few important lessons. "Now tell us again about the bear, Charlie."

"He was up on his hind legs, towering above me. Well, I couldn't think of what to do so I dropped and rolled, and then he sniffed me as if he was trying to figure out where to start eating. I was sure I was going to be breakfast, and imagined him chewing on me while I was still alive...remember the story of how that bear ate the miner up at Forty Mile? The poor man lived, but the bear chewed off his leg. I curled up for what seemed like forever and finally had enough nerve to look up to see his big butt moving away through the bush. I couldn't believe my luck!"

"Drop and roll is what you are supposed to do when your clothes are on fire," Victoria said.

"If it saved Charlie's life, then I am glad he was a little confused," Edward added.

"With all my book learning," Clara said, "I would not have survived if Uncle Joe hadn't rescued me. Charlie may have a different approach, but he was able to rescue himself and then help rescue Victoria."

"You should think about joining the force, my boy."

"If they feed me this well, maybe that would be a good profession. Could you pass the spuds, Clara?"

"Say please, Charlie. Always remember your manners," Victoria said with a smile.

"Hey, sis. Guess what? I missed your nagging when I was lost in the bush."

Yvonne Harris spent her childhood in the Yukon in the 1940s and '50s during the time of the paddlewheelers. She is an avid outdoors woman, even though a recent stroke has forced her to trade marathon canoeing for easy paddles. She has paddled the Yukon River at least 12 times beginning when her children were babies. Her youngest is now in her thirties. She told the story of the Echo Valley mystery to her children on one of her many trips on the Yukon River. The section of the river where the story is takes place has perfect echoes, thus the name of the wood camp. To write *Yukon Gold Mystery,* the author researched the Telegraph Trail, taking advantage of the excellent resources of the Yukon Heritage Branch and her colleagues from the Yukon Wildlife Branch.